*I Ain't Sayin'
She's A Gold
Digger*

I Ain't Sayin' She's A Gold Digger

Erica K. Barnes

www.urbanbooks.net

Urban Books, LLC
78 East Industry Court
Deer Park, NY 11729

I Ain't Sayin' She's a Gold Digger Copyright © 2008
Erica Barnes

ISBN 13: 978-1-60162-450-5
ISBN 10: 1-60162-450-6

First Mass Market Printing May 2011
First Trade Paperback Printing May 2008
Printed in the United States of America

10 9 8 7 6 5 4 3 2 1

*This is a work of fiction. Any references or similari-
ties to actual events, real people, living, or dead, or to
real locales are intended to give the novel a sense of
reality. Any similarity in other names, characters,
places, and incidents is entirely coincidental.*

Distributed by Kensington Publishing Corp.
Submit Wholesale Orders to:
Kensington Publishing Corp.
C/O Penguin Group (USA) Inc.
Attention: Order Processing
405 Murray Hill Parkway
East Rutherford, NJ 07073-2316
Phone: 1-800-526-0275
Fax: 1-800-227-9604

Acknowledgments

All praise and honor goes to my Lord and Savior Jesus Christ. Thank you for blessing me with my talents, moreover giving me each day to embrace them. Even though I fall short of giving You the glory, You continue to prove that You are all I need. If only I took the time out to truly bless You. . . .

Thank you, Mommy and Daddy, for supporting me. No words can describe your unconditional love! Thank you for putting up with my stubborn nature, teenage disrespect, and my "thought I knew it all" attitude! I'm learning . . . LOL! I love you so much!

Thank You, Thomas Colbert! You mean a lot to me and I thank God for putting you in my life. Even when you get on my last nerves, I wouldn't trade your love and friendship for anything.

Lastly, thank you to my new wonderful family at Q-Boro Books. Mark Anthony, Candace, Sabine, and my editor Tee C. Royal! I thank you from the bottom of my heart for giving this young author her shot.

Dedication

Dedicated to Stacey L. Cowan,
my best friend and god-sister!
Thank you for introducing writing to me
when we were little toddlers.
If we only knew how far it would carry us!

PART ONE:

$$*Kentia*
Bradford$$

Kentia Bradford

"Cuz the girls in the hood are always flyy.
You come talking that trash we'll black ya
eye.
Knowing nothing in life but to be the shit.
Don't quote me, boy, cuz I'm a flyy bitch."

My best friend Shanti and I rode down Slauson
Avenue singing our female version of Eazy-
E's classic West-Coast hit, "Boyz-N-The-Hood." We
bumped our heads to the beat and watched the
guys in neighboring cars give us the appealing eye.
Some tried to talk to us, but we ignored them like
conceited, snotty females who were too good to
give them conversation.

This Monday symbolized the first day of my
freedom. I had just graduated from Crenshaw High
School last Thursday and, boy, was I was glad. I
was happy to be in the presence of close friends
and family after the graduation, and Gradnight was
too much fun. Gradnight was the senior class trip
to Disneyland the night of graduation. Seniors from

different high schools across Southern California went to the happiest place on earth and enjoyed a night of youthful fun and celebrated their educational success.

Shanti had just picked me up from home and told me we were going shopping. Where and with what money were the two questions probing my mind. The money I had received as graduation gifts was spent at Disneyland, and the only thing resting in my wallet were some pictures and old movie ticket stubs. I was broke and in need of cash.

"Ooh, girl! I am so glad to be out of Crenshaw High! No more waking up at six in the morning and no more sitting in school for seven long hours! Girl, I am ready to party, on some real shit!" I said, as Shanti and I rode down the avenue.

"I heard that! Girl, I was so relieved when I graduated last year. I was high as hell too!" Shanti turned the stereo down so we could hear each other.

"Yeah," I remembered. "I'll never forget when you almost fell off the stage!"

"Oh my goodness, that was so embarrassing. Nobody will ever forget that. That shit made our graduation. To this day, everybody in class of '06 remembers my high ass walking along that edge, almost breaking my neck in the process. I shouldn't have smoked before graduation. I'll never live that down. However, it was kind of funny."

"Kind of funny? Girl, that was funny as hell!" I corrected.

"Fox Hills Mall or Crenshaw Mall?"

"Beverly Hills," I answered.

Shanti sucked her teeth and rolled her eyes. "When we get some Beverly Hills money then that's when we'll go. Girl, we are hood rich, if even that. I'm actually dead broke."

I laughed uneasily. "Yeah, you're right. Girl, I stopped making money after Baby Jon and I broke up, and now I'm broke. You and I both know for damn sure that Gertrude ain't giving me squat!"

Gertrude was my godmother, who willingly took me into her home after my mother went to jail for embezzlement. My father was a musician who was never a part of my life, and my other relatives lived outside of California. Although Gertrude gave me a place to stay, she felt that was all she had to do. She never gave me any money and did not feel obligated to. Because of that, I turned to selling weed to get money.

Shanti giggled and responded, "Kentia, she hasn't given you any money since you moved in with her. The most she's given you was a roof over your head and food. I'll give you your props, though. You made that li'l dope game work for you in high school. You was a top female hustler . . . selling that weed around the Shaw." She nodded her head in approval. "I taught you well."

I smiled when I thought about how I used to shine during my days at Crenshaw High. When Baby Jon and I were still together and going strong, I would get my weed from him and secretly sell it all around school. I would make up to five hundred a week with my nickel and dime bags. The game seemed easy, and that was all there was to it. Of course I kept my shit on me all the time, which was a risk in itself. But I'd rather it be that way than have a dog smell it in my locker when Crenshaw had a school-wide drug test.

People appreciated my business, and I realized that these people loved them some weed. You would only catch me selling that, though. No other kind of crazy drug. No crack, no meth, no angel dust, none of that other bullshit that had folks strung out of their minds. Weed was enough for me. After Baby Jon and I split up days before graduation, I found myself dead broke and in need of some money.

I convinced Shanti to go to the Beverly Center, even though we were broke. We went into the mall and became the epitome of window shoppers. There were items we wished we could purchase right then and there, but instead we were forced to make a mental note to come back and get it when we had some money in our wallets. I don't know how it affected Shanti, but all this "wishing-we-could-have-it" was encouraging me to get on my grind and make some money. What the grind would be was unknown. But I could sense it was coming in the near future.

When leaving the mall, Shanti came up with the suggestion that I'd just spend the night over her house. I was cool with that because I didn't want to be stuck at home. Now that I was out of school, I was ready to roam the city looking for fun. Shanti took me back to my house to get my stuff and I let Gertrude know what was up.

Gertrude was on the sofa reading the newspaper when we walked in. I acknowledged her. "Hey, God-Mommy," I said.

"Hey, *G*," Shanti said, abbreviating her name as she always did.

"Hello, Shanti. What are y'all getting into?" Gertrude asked.

"Kentia is going to spend the night over my house. We're just gonna hang out there because we don't have money to do nothing else. You cool with that?"

Gertrude nodded and stretched out on the couch. "Well, that's fine. Kentia, call me when you get to her house."

I nodded even though I knew I was not going to call her. I didn't know why Gertrude acted like she cared about my whereabouts, when she was so oblivious to everything going on in my life. I rolled my eyes and summoned Shanti into my room. It had been a long time since she had been in there. She looked around and saw how I had changed the place around. I had moved some furniture around and added a little entertainment system, all with the hard-earned weed money I made at Crenshaw.

I moved three composition notebooks off my bed and into the nightstand drawer. In each composition was a story I had started but never completed. That was how all the projects in my life seemed to be . . . futile.

A prime example of this was my relationship with Baby Jon. He was sweet, good-looking and had money. Being with him automatically put money in my pockets. However, I was bored with Baby Jon. In my mind, I felt there was someone better than him. My thinking was that there was always something better than what I currently had. Unfortunately, I was a walking double standard. In order to find that better something, you have to work for it. But I was lazy and didn't want to search.

Shanti paced over to my jewelry box and stood in awe at my collection. "Girl, this is too cute! Where did you get this from?" she asked, with much interest.

"I made this myself. You like it?" I asked, almost bragging.

"Kentia, I love it. Now that's where you can make some money. Girl, you should sell this stuff," Shanti suggested. "This is too flyy."

"Me? Sell jewelry? Girl, yeah right," I said skeptically.

"No, seriously. Bitches pay hundreds at the swap meet to get their jewelry. This stuff you got ain't bad-looking. Not bad-looking at all," Shanti said, holding up a pair of earrings to her ear. "Do you know how much you can make selling this stuff to the homegirls?"

I looked at her and said, "You got a point. All I use is my gold wire sculpting kit that Gertrude got me last Christmas. Been hooked on it ever since. You think I can get somewhere with that, huh?"

"Oh, girl, you can go far with this shit right here!" Shanti said excitedly.

"C'mon now, Shanti. Where am I gonna sell my products at?" I asked. It seemed as if I was turning her suggestion down, but I was really trying to see what ideas she could come up with next.

"You see them niggas on the corners of Crenshaw and Slauson selling everything from shoes to body oil? You better set up a spot and make that money."

Shanti was making sense. I knew I would make some money off of my jewelry. She wasn't the first person to compliment my work. Others had loved my unique designs too, and were interested in how I did it.

"Real shit though, I sho' nuff can take my ass to the corner and sell my jewelry. If they can buy them fake Louis Vuitton bags, then they can buy my shit." I laughed.

Shanti didn't laugh, but she agreed. "Girl, now that's wassup. Hustle real hard with that."

All the hustle talk was cracking me up with excitement. I became struck with the need for money and the need for success. If selling jewelry was my ticket away from being broke, then I was on it like white on rice.

I packed up and left with Shanti. That night we stayed up late watching movies and gorging on snacks. I went to bed with dreams of cash on my mind, and a come-up plan ready to be put into action.

A Few Weeks Later

Shanti was absolutely right! People in their cars noticed my setup and stopped to check out the latest entry to the Crenshaw corner hustle. Within time, word would spread and I'd be a money-making machine.

On my first day I had made a solid one-fifty. I figured that wasn't bad, being that it was day one. People started coming by the hour. For every time I gained a customer, I sold twice as much. Business was picking up faster than I could handle. I realized I'd have to go home and create some new and original jewelry to keep business thriving.

Within weeks of setting up my business, I realized that I had gotten honked at and hit on as much as I had sold my products. If I had five dollars per hit, I'd be making a thousand and more a day. It grossed me out when an old man tried to press up on me, but it turned me on when a sexy young cat did the same thing. But no matter who they were or where they came from, I turned down all offers because, at the moment, money was my man. Nobody was coming between that.

The most recent incident between men versus money occurred when a male friend of mine from Crenshaw High parked his car and got out to talk to me. I had noticed him from the Shaw and always thought he was sexy as hell but a straight-up asshole. He didn't realize exactly who I was until he got a closer look.

"Kentia Bradford! Baby Jon's girl," he said, surprised.

"Hey, Demari. Ain't seen you in a minute. And if you didn't know, I'm not with Baby Jon anymore, so you can cut all that out," I replied, tucking my hair behind my ears.

"Nah, leave your hair out. You look sexier like that," he said, pulling my hair back over my ears. "How you feel being out of school?"

"Happy as hell! You see I'm jumping straight into business. What about you?" I asked, rearranging some jewelry on display.

"I go to San Diego State in August," Demari replied.

"Word? What you tryin'a be in life?" I sat on the edge of the table.

"I have no idea. What are you tryin'a be?" Demari looked me up and down like I was a piece of meat and he was a hungry stray dog.

I replied, "A hustler."

"Aw damn," Demari sighed. "I thought you woulda wanted to be my girl."

"Demari, that was the wackest line ever. Don't ever say that to any girl. I'm being nice about it.

Any other girl would've shot you down with quickness," I told him truthfully.

"What kind of girl are you talking about? I done used that on plenty of females and it worked."

I gave him a sarcastic thumbs-up. "So are you tryin'a buy some jewelry for one of your hoes or what? I don't have time to talk. It's business with this bitch."

"Hoes? Girl, I ain't got no hoes. And you sell jewelry? What happened to the weed?" Demari asked.

I shrugged my shoulders. "It got thrown out the window when Baby Jon and I broke up. What do you want? Earrings? Necklace? Bracelet?"

Demari shook his head. "Nah, I got enough ice on for now, mami." He lifted his chain. It was glistening with diamonds as the sun reflected off of it. "I bet you if you were my girl you wouldn't be out here on this corner tryin'a hustle."

"I don't want to make that bet. And *tryin'a* hustle, Demari? Nigga, I *am* hustling. Get that straight right now, alright? I'm making a nice stack of paper doing what I'm doing," I defended.

Demari chuckled. "Chill out, Kentia. I feel you, trust me, I do. I know you out here doing your thing. All I'm saying is, let me be the one to spoil you, girl. I can hook you up with whatever you want every now and then."

The thought of Demari being my money well was nice, but I had too much independence and confidence with the hustle I had going on right now. I shook my head and replied, "Sorry, Demari. This chick is good on you. But don't you worry. I'm sure you can use one of your pickup lines and catch another girl off guard. But, me, I always got my guard up. Good luck hunting."

"Come on, baby girl. Seriously, how much money are you making from selling jewelry on the corner? You know if you needed anything, I got you."

"Yeah, that sounds good, but where the hell are you getting your money from? And aren't you going to school? You got shit to pay for, right?" I asked him. "It ain't like you selling drugs or nothing."

I knew Demari was a pretty boy who wouldn't go near anything that would get him thrown in jail. He wasn't making money, his parents were. It would never work out between me and him.

Demari rolled his eyes and walked back to his car parked in the gas station behind me. He looked upset, like his ego was hurt. I didn't really care. It was just another case of M.O.N.—Money Over Niggas. All day, every day.

But just like Biggie said, "Mo' money mo' problems." I could see the problems arising, starting with the body oil man across the street. He had been on his corner for about a year strong and was doing average. I was pretty damn sure business didn't pick up as fast for him as it did for me. Jealousy was expected, and I was ready to play defense.

He crossed the street and walked over to my table to see how business was picking up for me.

"What's good, man?" I asked him, trying to be nice.

I could see the jealousy in his eyes. I wanted to tell him not to hate the player, hate the game. He could hate the fact that I was winning, but it wasn't my fault that the game was in my favor. It also wasn't my fault that city folk didn't want his body oils. They were probably tired of breaking out after rubbing it on. I could use that to his demise. I knew he was scoping me out to see who and what the competition was.

"Oh, nothing really. Just looking to see if my wife would like some of the jewelry you're sell-ing," he answered, looking over my products.

"Then bring her here and let her see," I replied.

"I'm going to have to," he said. "How does it feel to be a part of the hustle here on Crenshaw Boulevard? You tryin'a make that money, huh? You're a real pretty li'l thing. What brings you to the street to sell?"

I rolled my eyes. "Nah, homie, I been a part of the hustle. I'm just now getting on Crenshaw."

"Really?" he asked. "You sell this in school?"

"I ain't in school, brothaman. I graduated al-most a month ago," I said. "You might want to go over to your spot. I'm running a business and cus-tomers are waiting for my service."

I turned toward the two women who were wait-ing for me.

"I know that's right!" one of the two said. "Peace out, Mr. Body Oil." She giggled with her friend as he walked away angrily.

"Girl," began the second friend, "he got some nerve coming over here. You know he just being nosey cuz he ain't got no customers coming his way. Over here is where it's at. Your li'l jewelry is too cute."

I nodded my head in appreciation. "Thank you,

girl. What can I get you today, ladies?" I showed them the newest pieces to my collection.

"How much is this bracelet?" the first girl asked, picking it up and trying it on.

"Girl, that one is five, but I got a two-for-seven special especially for y'all," I said pointing at other pieces I thought they would personally like.

"Well, let me get this one here, Tishana, and I'll pay you back," the second girl said, picking up the necklace she'd had her eye on since she first looked at the jewelry on the table. She tried it on.

I collected the money and continued running business with the customers behind them. I felt I had done pretty damn well for dodging bullets from the body oil man. As long as business kept doing well and I kept making money, I could care less how he felt about me.

Oh, My God-brother!

Living with my godmother Gertrude was a trip. She was an old Southern Belle who relocated to LA from Alabama back in the 1960s to escape harsh racism. She had a thirty-two-year-old daughter named Bernice, a twenty-five-year-old son named Prince, and a nineteen-year-old son, who was also my best friend.

His name was Corey. He was a football player at USC on a full scholarship, and had graduated from Crenshaw with honors. Way to beat the hood! He never got involved in gangs, even though almost all of his friends were Crips from the surrounding neighborhoods. Corey stayed far away from drugs, gangs, and money-hungry girls. He had been with his devoted girlfriend Robin since the eighth grade. They won homecoming and prom king and queen their senior year back in 2003. Robin had proven herself worthy of Corey's love and became the number three girl in his heart, after his mother and me.

Corey was on his way to future success and didn't have the hood watching him in envy. They were honored and proud of him for being a somebody. He was a role model to younglings in the neighborhood. Every time he came back from USC, he would pay them a visit to see how they were doing and make sure they were staying out of trouble.

I was proud to have him as my godbrother and had the utmost respect for him. He knew of my financial situation and did his best to help me with cash in every way. Believe me . . . five and ten dollars went a long way in my pocket. I admired Corey, but could never be him.

Corey made an unexpected visit home and found me lounged on the sofa watching the Game Show Network.

"CO-REEEEY!" I screeched as I jumped to my feet and tackled him in a hug. "What are you doing here?"

"Robin wanted to see me since we haven't hooked up in almost two weeks. But I decided to stop by the house," he said, sitting up on the floor. "What you been up to, sis?"

"I'm chilling. Glad to be out of school, but hate being the two *B*'s," I replied.

Corey was confused. "The two *B*'s?"

"Broke and bored."

"You ain't broke," Corey responded after sucking his teeth.

"Why would you say that?" I was shocked.

"Man, Robin told me she seen you on the Crenshaw corner. How is that coming?"

"It's alright," I answered as humbly as I could,

when I really wanted to brag like hell about my business. "Damn, Robin couldn't even stop buy and support me?" I laughed.

"So your business is just *alright*?" he asked. "But I see it bought you those Jordans and those Rock and Republic jeans."

"I worked for them, though." I giggled.

"Well, at least you ain't selling weed."

I was surprised. "You knew about that?"

"Yeah, I did. You know the li'l homies you sold to at Crenshaw told me all the info. You were supposedly the number one supplier in the ghetto yearbook," Corey answered.

"Damn, and I called myself being sneaky," I said. "Baby Jon beat me by winning the number one hustler."

Corey laughed. "You are crazy. I'm pretty sure the other corner boys are mad that you're getting a lot of customers."

"Hell yeah, cuz, I'm making that paper! Body Oil Man had the nerve to come over to my spot and check out my shit," I informed him.

"That's too funny. I know you went off on him," Corey said.

"Nope, I didn't!" I said, surprised at myself when remembering how things went down. "I held it down and didn't even have to get loud. But he better know where I'm coming from."

"He is a trip. Don't pay him no mind. Keep on doing what you're doing, li'l sis," Corey said. "Is Mom home?"

"Nope, not yet," I answered. "What are you and Robin going to do?"

"She's been talking about Denzel Washington's movie," Corey answered. "We might hit up the movies."

"All right. If she calls, you want me to tell her you stopped by?" I asked, sitting back on the couch.

"Could you please? Tell her I'm on my way." Corey got up and started walking toward the door. "Talk to you later, Kentia. Call me if you need anything."

"You know I will," I said, adding a slick grin.

Corey chuckled and left the house.

I tuned back into my game show. The house phone rang, getting me out of game show mood. I answered the phone.

"Hello?" I asked politely, just in case it was somebody for Gertrude.

"Kentia?" the female voice asked.

"Yeah, who's this?" I asked, still in polite mode.

"Girl, this is Robin. Why you talking like a white woman? Where's the ghetto girl in you?" Robin joked.

"Right hurrr!" I screeched. I laughed and continued, "What up with you?"

"Nothing, just chilling. Did my man stop by yet?"

"Yeah, girl, he's on his way over there right now as we speak. We were just talking about you, Robin," I answered.

"Oh, for real? What was said?" Robin asked.

"Nothing really. He just told me you saw me on Crenshaw and Slauson," I replied. "I'm mad that you didn't want to stop by and see what I was selling."

"Girl, me and Ronelle was in a rush that day. I

just happened to look to my left and saw you there. I'm sorry, girl. Just for that, I'm going to stop buy tomorrow and buy something. That's my word," Robin replied.

"Aw, that's so nice, Robin. But don't make it a promise, because I'm gonna be real mad if you don't show up," I said.

"Don't hold it against me, Kentia," Robin replied, laughing. "I'm going to try to come through."

"Don't worry about it," I answered, and really meant it. I had enough customers who bought my jewelry.

"I'll try my best to stop by," she answered. "All right, let me go get ready to see my man!" She sounded excited, and I'm pretty damn sure she was.

Oh, Hell Nah!

Late into the afternoon, around two o'clock, I began setting up my table. I was running late big time. I should've been rolling by ten. I could feel the body oil man's eyes watching me as I hastily set up. I regretted staying out later the night before. Shanti had picked me up and we went to her cousin Taffy's house. We had a little party with him and two of his boys and smoked till dawn. I didn't get home till five in the morning. I should've just stayed my ass at home and caught up on sleep, but money was money, and it needed to be made. Besides, it would be a busy afternoon, which meant money in my pocket.

The delay allowed me to catch the kid crowd. It was just in time to get the students from Crenshaw High and View Park Prep right after school let out. By three o'clock, teenagers were scoping out my products and buying what they liked. I couldn't believe I was about to sell out. Business didn't end. Around five-thirty, the next wave of working people came and hit up whatever was left.

"Damn, I'm ballin," I admitted to myself. I discreetly counted my cash. ". . . four-sixty, four-eighty . . . damn, almost five hundred." I stuffed about three hundred in my bra and kept the rest in my pocket.

This was the first time I had sold out completely, and I was glad about it. I called Shanti and told her I had sold out. I asked her to come pick me up, something she had done faithfully since the first day I started selling my jewelry.

"Girl, you sold out completely! Now where is my cut of the cash? I was the one who gave you this ingenious idea!" Shanti said.

I giggled. "Girl, I got you. Just come get me. I want to go shopping!"

"All right," Shanti said. "I'm on the way now, girl."

I breathed a sigh of relief and began thinking about ways to take my hustle to the next level. I didn't want to be stuck on the corner long term. Although it brought me good money, I didn't want to sell jewelry forever. Just like with everything else, I knew there was something better than this. I didn't know what it was, but I figured the more I thought about it, the more it would make itself clear.

Out of nowhere, I was hit in the head with a heavy fist. I fell to the ground in agony and pain. Someone began to stomp the hell out of me. My body grew numb to the pain of a large Timberland boot jamming into my side. I lay helplessly on the ground as two pair of hands searched my body for money. Unfortunately, the money in my pocket was found and stolen. They stopped the robbery and ran away. I slowly got up and saw them hop into the getaway car waiting in the middle of Crenshaw, blocking traffic. The car zoomed off.

"OH HELL NAH!" I screamed angrily.

At least they didn't get all of it, I thought as I commended myself for secretly hiding the majority of the money in my bra. I was pissed the hell off because I thought that all these city people would have seen what was happening and tried to stop it. Then again, I didn't blame them because they could've got their ass jacked up if they interfered.

I wiped the blood away from my busted lip with the corner of my shirt. "Shit!" I cursed. "WHAT THE FUCK YOU LOOKIN' AT?" I yelled at the incense-selling Jamaican standing on the median of Crenshaw.

He quickly turned away. The bootlegging couple set up in front of Louisiana Fried Chicken ran across the street to see if I was okay. Finally, somebody was concerned and sincere.

"I'm alright," I said, thankful for their concern.

"Look at Jimmy," the woman said. "Over there still selling his oils as if nothing happened."

"He got some nerve!" her partner said.

"Honey, get back over to our table before somebody steals our stuff!" she yelled. She looked at me as her partner crossed over Slauson Avenue. She thought I would get mad at her bringing up the word *steal*, nothing would be able to take back me getting robbed.

"Is someone coming to get you?" she asked, taking out a tissue from her purse. She handed it to me and I wiped the side of my mouth with it.

I nodded my head. "Yeah, my friend is on her way right now."

Five minutes later, Robin pulled up alongside the curb. "Girl, you not selling anymore today?" she asked with her money in her hand. She was ready to buy.

"Nah, girl, I sold out and I got robbed!" I said, still angry with what just happened. "It happened so fast, and I didn't even see it coming."

Robin shook her head. "Girl, you want me to call Corey? You know he'll be here in a heartbeat!"

I shook my head. "Nah, girl, don't bring him into this. I don't know who did it. The people who robbed me had on masks. Damn, that shit is foul!" I put my hands on my waist and took a deep breath. Exhaled. "I can't believe I, of all people, got robbed!"

"Kentia, bad stuff happens to the best of us. Don't trip, though, you'll be alright. You got a ride home?" Robin asked, putting one arm around me.

"Yeah, Shanti is on her way now."

"All right, girl," Robin said, looking toward her car. "Did they take a lot of money?"

"They only got about two hundred," I answered.

Robin ran back over to me and gave me her twenty. "Here, girl, don't trip. Shit will work out for you," she said. She turned around and walked toward her car.

I smiled and felt glad to know somebody as sweet as Robin.

Changing Plans

After I told Shanti all the details about the broad daylight robbery, she was heated. She was more ticked off than I was. She was ready to get Taffy and have him handle the body oil man, all because she thought he had something to do with it.

"Girl, don't even trip. I'm good," I replied. "Everything is gonna be okay."

"Kentia, you're a good one. Let that have been my ass, and I would've shot up the incense guy, the body oil man, and the bootleggers! Hell, I woulda shot up everything up and down Crenshaw! Hell nah!" Shanti said.

"Girl, you acting like you the one that got robbed." I giggled, trying to find some humor in this situation. I grew calm. Quietly I said, "Damn, now what am I gonna do?" I got up and approached the mirror to see how busted up I was.

"Are you going to find another corner to sell on?" Shanti asked. "That's always an option."

"Bitch, I am not going back to the corner. What the fuck do I look like?"

"You look like a bitch in need of a damn job. Why don't you just get a job working somewhere like me?" Shanti asked.

I rolled my eyes. "You sound like Gertrude. It ain't that easy. And I tried working at certain places . . . I don't like it. I wanna be my own boss."

"Forget the corner hustle. My uncle Theo has a booth in the Slauson Swap Meet. I can talk to him and see if he can let you sell from there," Shanti said.

"Didn't I just say that I want to be my own boss?" I asked her, the attitude in my voice apparent.

"Stop being a stubborn bitch. You got any other ideas?" Shanti asked.

"All right, I guess that'll have to do," I said reluctantly.

Shanti sucked her teeth. "Pssht! Have to do? Kentia, that's the only thing that will do. If you don't work there, then you'll be broke."

I hated the truth about my predicament. All I could do was accept what I had gotten into and try to rise above it.

Shanti whipped out her cell phone and dialed her uncle Theo's number.

"Uncle Theo!" she howled when he answered the phone. She put it on speaker, so I could be in on the conversation.

"Hey, baby girl," Theo replied. "How are you?"

"Living," Shanti said. "How's Aunt Amber?"

Theo responded, "She's good, and the baby is fine too."

"I was just about to ask that," Shanti said. "But, yes, I need a favor."

"Anything, my favorite niece," Theo answered.

Shanti looked at me and began, "A friend of mine has a business selling jewelry. She brings in a lot of profit, Theo, no lie. She was selling on the corner of Crenshaw and Slauson, but this afternoon she got robbed."

"In broad daylight?" Theo asked, more interested in me getting robbed than me being a young entrepreneur.

"Yes, broad daylight," Shanti continued. "But she doesn't want to return to the corner because she's scared she'll get robbed again."

I sucked my teeth. Shanti looked at me and waved her finger. Obviously, she knew what she was doing. It was her uncle, not mine. She knew how to work him.

"I told her about you and your booth in the swap meet. Is it okay if she sells her jewelry from your booth? It'll bring in some new customers," Shanti proposed.

Uncle Theo was all for it. "Um, sure, I guess. Ask her if she can start next Monday. Come in with her so you can show her where I'm at."

"Of course I'm going to come in with her, Uncle Theo," Shanti said.

"Tell her I'm sorry for her, but everything will be okay at the swap meet. They got more security in there than the LAPD county jail," he joked.

Shanti laughed. "Okay, Uncle Theo, I will. Bye-bye." She hung up the phone. "And just like that, girl, you're in there! See how simple that was? Now you get time over the weekend to make some new jewelry and shit, so you can return to business on Monday."

My cell phone began ringing. It was Corey. I guessed Robin told him about the robbery. I was ready to hear an angry Corey. I answered the phone.

"Hey, brother," I replied.

"Who did it? Why didn't you fight back, Kentia?" Corey asked in a rampage.

"Brother," I said. "Don't worry about it. They didn't take all of my money. I'm not even tripping. Did Robin tell you?"

"Hell yeah, she told me," Corey answered. "You shoulda had a guy with you. Someone like a body-guard, you know what I'm saying?"

"Yes, Corey, I do know what you're saying. Shanti thinks the body oil man had something to do with it," I said.

"The body oil man did it? That's it! I'm 'bout to pay his ass a visit tomorrow," Corey said angrily.

"Corey, I said she *thinks*! We don't know if it's for sure. And what are you gonna do? Challenge his ass to a game of football? Just leave it alone, okay, Corey?"

"Kentia, you need to be safe and secure with whatever you are doing."

"Don't you think I know that?"

"You aren't acting like it."

"You think I asked to get robbed?" I asked. "Damn, Corey. Can we just leave it alone? I get upset thinking about it."

"Fine. I'll leave it alone. When are you coming home?"

"Soon. I'm going to get something to eat."

"All right. Call me when you get in."

"I will. Love you!"

"Love you too, sis."

We got off the phone.

Before Shanti took me home, we went to Panda Express in the Baldwin Hills Crenshaw Mall to get some Chinese food. I was yearning for some Kung Pao chicken after a day like this.

Welcome to the
Swap Meet

Monday was day number one of me working at the Slauson Swap Meet. It was ironic to me because most of the booth owners in the Slauson Swap Meet, as in other swap meets across South Central, were of Asian descent. It was to no surprise that Uncle Theo was good friends with the Asians all up and through the place. Shanti and I walked in on the morning conversation between Theo and one of the fellow workers.

"Morning, Theo!" the Korean man said.

"Hey, Jin-Shin!" Theo greeted merrily. "How are you?"

"I do good, I do good!" His broken English was apparent in his speech. "You hear news 'bout my country?"

"Um . . . Japan? Oh, yeah, man, read it in the newspaper," Theo lied.

"No, fool! I not Japanese! I'm South Korean! You know dat! You know dat!" he said, throwing his hands in the air. "What wrong wit you?"

"Sorry, man," Theo replied. He turned and saw

Shanti and me approaching. "Hey, girls. Hello, Kentia." He shook my hand. "Jin-Shin! I want you to meet one of my new employees, Kentia."

He says employees, *like I was hired or some shit*, I thought. "Hello," I said quietly, putting on that shy-girl act.

"Hi, Kentia. I Jin-Shin Ho," he replied. "You very pretty. How dey say it? You da bomb!"

"Nobody says *the bomb* anymore," Theo told Jin-Shin. "Come on, let me show you where you can set up, my dear."

After Theo introduced me to my new space, he began the talk about rent. "On average, how much were you making a week?"

"Like four hundred," I lied, bringing down the actual number by a hundred.

"Four hundred, eh?" Theo said.

What? You don't believe me? I thought. "Yes, four hundred."

"So you know there is rent for the space, right?"

For one fuckin' fourth of your store? No, this nigga didn't, I thought. "I know now. So how much is rent?"

Theo looked upward and did the math in his head. "Seventy five every two weeks."

"So one fifty a month?"

Theo nodded his head. "All right. You can set up now. I'm going to work on getting you a sign to advertise."

I flashed him a phony smile as if I was really happy. Honestly, I was not excited. Deep down I knew I could be doing something more rewarding and certainly more exciting than selling jewelry in the swap meet. Until I knew what that something was, though, I was going to do what I had to do to keep money in my pocket.

I set up and began my little business. It picked up occasionally, but not as much as it did outside on the corner.

After weeks of working at the swap meet, I had my share of customers. If I could take business from when I was selling on Crenshaw and Slauson and put it inside the swap meet, I would. Everything would be twice as good.

There was one thing that didn't slide too far down. That was the number of times I got hit on. It became more annoying than flattering. As cute as they were, I never got the numbers of any of the guys who made passes at me. For one, if I was going to talk to you, I didn't want you doing your daily shopping at the swap meet . . . and some of these guys were making too many visits a week. It was already a hassle trying to sneak past the Muslim brothers reppin' the Nation of Islam in front of all the entrances and exits of the swap meet. Having to deal with these thugs trying to make passes at me only added to the problem.

On one particular Wednesday, I had gone on my third break of the day and went to the nearest jewelry spot to buy my fifth pair of bamboo earrings. Every West Coast chick should have a gold pair of bamboo earrings, preferably big. I had the heart-shaped ones, a big pair with my name in the middle, the heart-shaped ones with BITCH in the middle, a smaller pair, and now I was going to buy lucky number five.

Cynthia, the prettiest Mexican girl one could ever meet, was working this hour, lucky for me.

Her turquoise contacts sparkled under the light as she looked at me coming over. She stopped playing with her curly and wet-looking hair and waved.

"Hey, Cynthia," I said as I leaned on the giant glass case.

"Hey, *chica*, what's up?" she asked.

"Ready to purchase some more earrings. How much are these?" I pointed to the desired earrings in the glass case.

"I think these are one-twenty, I'm not sure. But I can hook you up with them for eighty," Cynthia said, taking them out of the case.

"Oh, that's wassup. Let me get them." I peeled off eighty dollars for her. "I see you got yours in. Name in the middle and everything."

"Yes, girl. Cute, huh?"

"Really cute," I said, taking my earrings and putting them in. "How do I look?"

"Sexy as hell," the deep voice behind me said.

I looked at Cynthia. She looked at the guy, and then at me. She smiled with her eyes, telling me he was attractive. I turned around and looked at his shoes first. He had on a clean pair of Nike Dunks. The colors were original, so he had better be matching to the tee. His jeans were vintage, looking like something out of an exclusive boutique on Sunset. He wore a hoodie that matched his Dunks. He was fresh and clean, just how I liked my men.

Sexy was the thought in my mind when I saw his face. He had that baby-face appeal. Brown skin, almond-shaped light-brown eyes, fresh fade and a little facial hair, giving him a baby face with a grown man's touch. But he wouldn't be going far because he was here at the Slauson Swap Meet.

For what? I didn't know, and I didn't care. It was a wrap.

"What's your name, sexy?" he asked.

"Kentia," I answered.

He stuck his hand out and I shook it. He introduced himself as Dante. He was twenty-one. I told him my tender age of eighteen and he almost became hesitant to talk to me. He figured I wasn't on his grown level. I was obviously too sexy to let go, so he asked for my number.

"Nah, I can't do that," I replied. I turned my back on him and faced Cynthia.

Cynthia gasped and turned around. She must've found it hard to believe I didn't want to take this offer. She pretended to be tuned into her Spanish soap operas on the 16-inch television.

"Ah, for real? Why not though?" Dante asked.

"I ain't interested in a brotha who is shopping at the swap meet. One pair of shoes is good, maybe even a shirt," I said honestly. "But for the most part, I'm good."

"Almost too good, huh?" Dante laughed. He looked at Cynthia and shook his head. "Oh, okay then," he said, still chuckling. "Well, excuse me while I do business."

I moved out of his way and watched him approach Cynthia.

"She didn't mean it," Cynthia said, looking at me with disappointment in her eyes.

"Give her my number anyway," Dante mumbled.

"All right," Cynthia agreed. "Hold on while I go back to get it." She knew Dante's original intent. She went to the back and came back out with three jewelry cases. She bagged them up and handed it to him.

"Thanks, Cynthia. Tell Hector I said wassup." Dante then nodded his head at me and walked away.

I looked at Cynthia. She frowned at me and shook her head. "Bitch, don't look at me like that!" I joked. "You know him!"

Cynthia nodded. "Yeah, I know him, stupid! Your ass missed out on a real good opportunity. Dante only comes in here to see me. Hector is his weed man."

"His supplier? Or somebody he buys weed from to smoke?" I asked.

"Supplier, Kentia. Don't say shit though. Hector would beat my ass," Cynthia said.

"Who am I going to tell?" I asked. "Why didn't you say something sooner?" I nudged her in her arm playfully.

"I don't know! I didn't know you was turning guys down just because they step foot in the swap meet," Cynthia answered.

I laughed. "Yeah, that does make me a little evil bitch, huh?"

"Your values, not mine," Cynthia said.

I asked her, "So, what do you know about Dante?"

"I know that boy is BALLIN'! Girl, Hector told me he got money in the bank because only the truest dealers fuck with my boo," Cynthia said. "He from Watts, and I ain't sure about this, but he's supposedly a Crip from six-oh, girl."

"A Crip, huh?" I bit my bottom lip.

"He better be, if he messing with Hector. You

know Hector don't get down with no Bloods," Cynthia said.

"Cynthia," I began, "I'm surprised he supplies to the Blacks period. You know the beef Mexicans and Blacks got in LA."

Cynthia nodded her head. "Yeah, but it don't bother him much. Hector is mad coo' with black people." She giggled. "But Dante is one of a kind. You know he got his hoes. He with another female every time he comes to our house."

"Hector ever took you around where he stays?" I asked.

"He stays on West and Sixty-third. I hate going around there, girl. One time, I had to pick Hector up from there. Girl, I thought these guys were about to jump me and jack me for my ride. They were mugging me so viciously!" Cynthia laughed.

I shook my head. "Not with you being Hector's girl. Shit, you know Hector and his people will be all up in they ass," I told her.

Cynthia nodded. She knew it was true. She gave me Dante's number. I planned to give him a call soon.

Getting Dante

I woke up around three o'clock on a Saturday afternoon. Lucky for me, I wouldn't be at the swap meet selling jewelry from Theo's booth. It was my day off, and boy, was I going to chill. I was so tired and out of place from last night. Once again, I was up till the wee hours of the morning partying with Shanti, Taffy, and his boys. We got high as hell and drunk as I don't know what.

I looked at my cell phone and saw there were six missed calls. Two from Shanti, one from Corey, one from Cynthia, and two from Baby Jon. I didn't return any calls. I browsed through my phone book and dialed Dante's number. The phone rang and I hung up after the third ring. I got up and got ready for what was left of the day.

A private number was calling my cell phone. I answered, "What's up?"

"Who is this?" the man's voice said.

I recognized the voice from the swap meet. "Dante?"

"Who is this?" he repeated his question again.

"This is Kentia. Cynthia's friend," I replied.

"The one who turned me down at the swap meet?" Dante replied. "Oh word. What's up? Cynthia gave you my number?"

"Yeah, she did. How are you?" I asked, trying to sound friendly, when I really wanted to ask him when we were going to go shopping.

"Good, and you?" Dante asked, gentleman-like.

"Tired. I was out late," I answered. "Are you doing something today?"

"Don't have shit planned. I'll probably just hang out at the crib or go over my boy's house," Dante answered.

"Where you stay at?" I asked, even though I already knew the answer.

"You asking a lot of questions, Kentia," Dante replied.

"Oh, is that a problem?" I asked, getting an attitude. *No, this nigga didn't,* I thought.

Dante replied, "Chill, Kentia. I didn't mean it like that. I just don't like talking over the phone. I'd rather talk in person. You want to get together tonight?"

"Where we going?".

"How about the Grand Lux over in Beverly Hills?" Dante asked. "Dinner on me."

Grand Lux, I thought. *That must mean this dude got money. Oh, he is a keeper.* "All right, what time do you plan to leave out?" I asked.

Dante paused and thought of a good time. "Can I come pick you up 'round seven-thirty?"

I looked at the time. "That's a good time."

"Where do you stay at?"

"On Ninth and Fifty-fourth," I answered.

"Over by Crenshaw High?"

"Yup."

I gave him further directions and began getting ready for our date. Just as he said, seven-thirty approached and Dante was in front of my crib. I came out looking stunning in a black bebe dress, gold sandals, and matching gold accessories.

I fell in love with Dante's luxurious ride, a 2006 Benz SL that had money written all over it. I got in and smelled the fresh leather. I gave him a hug. He had the nerve to turn to 94.7 The Wave, playing the best in smooth jazz. I guess he was trying to get into character, which was alright with me. I tried not to laugh as he nodded his head to the upbeat jazz playing on the radio.

"What's the matter? You don't listen to jazz?" he asked as we headed toward Beverly Hills.

"Not really," I replied. "But it's your car and your radio. I can manage."

Once we arrived at the Grand Lux, Dante kept the gentleman act going. He opened the car door for me and opened the doors to the Grand Lux. He told me to sit and wait while he checked in with the waiter for our reservations. I was surprised to see the waiter recognized him.

"Hey there, Dante. How's it going?" he asked cheerfully.

"Everything is good, Abram. What about you, my friend?" Dante asked, shaking the waiter's hand.

"Great. My father asked about you not too long ago. You got to pay us a visit sometime soon, alright?" Abram said.

"I will do that. Reservations for two, Abram."

"I see you, come on. I'll take you to a table right now," Abram said, grabbing two menus.

Dante grabbed my hand, and we followed Abram to our booth, toward the back of the restaurant. It was nice and secluded . . . just how I wanted things to be for this date with Dante.

"Abram, this is my lovely date for the evening, Kentia. Kentia, this is my good friend Abram. His father designed a chain for me at his jeweler's shop."

"Hello," Abram said, taking my hand and kissing it. "Lovely lady, Dante. Very lovely. Nice to meet you, Kentia."

"Nice to meet you, too" I said, flattered at his courtesy.

"You haven't been here in a long time, Dante. What's been going on?" said the over-friendly Abram.

"Man, tryin'a get things straight. It's crazy in my neck of the woods," Dante said. "Finally got my mom out of Watts and moved her into a home in Granada Hills. My aunt, her sister, stays out there, and was trying to get her to move out there for the longest time."

"Get her out the ghetto, huh? I feel you, man," Abram said.

"Come on, Abram," Dante said. "What do you know about the ghettos?"

"Dante, I'm Jewish. I know all about the ghettos," Abram joked.

We laughed.

"All right, let me stop clowning around. Can I start you all out with some drinks?"

"I'll take tequila with lime," Dante said.

"I'd like a virgin margarita," I ordered.

Abram left us alone at the table.

Dante began the conversation. "A virgin margarita? Why not all the way?"

"I'm only eighteen, remember?" I asked, smiling. "So, Dante, tell me why you're single. You seem to be the perfect gentleman, and no girl has won your heart over?"

Dante shook his head. "I don't know. To be honest, I haven't been looking for the one. I'm young, and I'm not ready to love a girl *half* way. If I fall in love, it's going to be all the way."

This is your lucky day, cuz this bitch ain't looking for love either, I thought. A smile spread across my face. I replied, "That's too crazy because I feel that exact same way. Now I've been in my long relationships. In fact, my last boyfriend and I were together for a year and half, but things just didn't work out the way I thought they would. Ever since then, I've been scared to love." *This "afraid-to-open-my-heart" deal should be a shoo-in for me.*

"Well, what happened with your last boyfriend?" Dante asked, now interested in my past.

I lied and said, "My last boyfriend really didn't give a damn about me. I tried to be the perfect girl and give him everything he wanted. I sacrificed so much and got nothing in return. It really hurts when you love someone, but they don't love you back. You probably think I'm too mushy now, don't you?"

"No, not at all," Dante said. "In fact, I like a girl that can open up to me. It lets me know they're real."

Yeah, real scandalous, I thought. *Dante, you have absolutely no idea what you're getting yourself into.* "Well, I hope I'm not scaring you off or anything. But I get really sensitive when it comes to topics like this because I've been hurt. Do you know what it feels like to be hurt, Dante?"

"No, can't say that I do," Dante said, shaking his head. "I know what it feels like to hurt someone, unfortunately."

"Oh, at least you can admit it," I said. *Well, pretty soon you're gonna be hurting, out of your pockets!*

"Yeah," Dante said. "So, since we both aren't so down for automatically falling in love, how about we start things off slow with a little dating every now and then?"

"You got yourself a deal."

"I do have to tell you one thing, though," Dante began, "I do love to spoil the woman I'm with, especially if she is as sexy as you."

"Oh really? Is that your way of getting the pussy?" I said in blunt honesty. If it was, I knew which game to play and if it wasn't, things would run even smoother for me.

"Girl, please! All the ladies I've been with have given that up on their own free will. Not to sound conceited or anything, but I'm addictive," he said, rubbing his chin with his index and middle finger.

I sucked my teeth and said, "You sound very conceited saying that. How long is it before the female decides to let you hit it?"

"Probably about a week or two," Dante said.

Now that was what I had to top. I had to make Dante hold out longer than a week (or two), plus more. I knew there was risk involved, because Dante could just easily drop me for not letting him hit. But if he was the guy I thought he was, he would hold onto me in hopes of getting me in his bed.

The rest of the date was spent conversing about our past, our future goals, and materialism. I had Dante thinking I was the girl who was skeptical about relationships and now devoted her time to starting a jewelry business, when in actuality I could not stand being in relationships and I was all about the money.

I left the date feeling I had won Dante over by fooling him into thinking I was the perfect girl.

After three weeks, as expected, Dante took things to the next level and asked me to be his girl. And get this: I still hadn't let him hit it. I didn't let him hit it for months. During those months I played the innocent-girl role. I acted as if I was doubtful about being with him and really made an effort to trust him. He tried to buy my love with those oh-so-fabulous designers like Christian Dior, Dolce and Gabbana, Versace, and Louis Vuitton— just to name a few—I was sure he was fucking other girls on the side to ease his hormone cravings, but I wasn't worried. As long as I was getting my share of his money, everything was in my control.

When I finally did let him hit seven months into our relationship, I cursed myself for waiting so damn long. Dante had that good dick, the kind that made a girl walk funny for the whole day after she got some. However, the good sex didn't overrule the fact that I was only with him for the money.

During the seven months, he had never given me money, in terms of bills. He bought me very luxurious gifts. I never took the tags off—he left them on to make sure I saw how much the item was—and found the receipts in his drawers. I would return the gifts I didn't care for. Already, I knew in my head that I would not be doing this forever.

I was working my way to becoming a gold digger . . . and that was that.

The Ballers' Party

Dante didn't break me off with cash, only things that a lot of cash bought. I became bored with him physically and financially. It was time to move on to bigger and better ballers.

I expressed my feelings to Shanti, who I believed would have a solution to my problem. "Dante is getting pointless to me. I want money to get what I want. He comes in here with gifts for me . . . some I like, some I don't like. I return the ones I don't like. That's how I get extra money, aside from selling jewelry."

"Okay?" Shanti asked as if she didn't see the problem.

"I can care less about gifts. I want the money, girl. Dante doesn't do that. I want to get to the point where I can stop making jewelry and selling it. You know what I mean?" I replied. "Like, I know for a fact there are them niggas that can give their girls a couple of hundreds like it's nothing. I want that nigga."

Shanti smiled. "You must have been introduced to Dante's homies, huh?"

I giggled. "How did you know?"

"'Cuz you got exposed to better."

"All his homies are sexy as hell. Girl, the only thing that stopped me from talking to them was the fact that Dante was right by my side," I said, thinking about the friends I'd met over me and Dante's eight-month relationship.

Once again, Shanti came up with a genius plan. She told me the smooth way to get to some of the A-List hustlers Dante was close to.

"All right, check this shit out," Shanti began. "You need to convince his ass to throw a party for only the top-flight hustlers. Meet them there and work them afterwards."

Her suggestion appealed to the mind's eye. I was definitely running with it.

That same night, I came to Dante with the proposal. "Baby, we should throw one huge party for the real hustlers in these streets and the flyyest bitches, too!"

Dante looked at me. "Kentia, get your things, 'cuz I'm about to take you home," he said, ignoring what I had just said.

"DANTE!" I exclaimed. "You don't like my idea? C'mon, it'll be hot, boo!"

Dante looked at me and rolled his eyes. "Girl, you must be crazy to think I'm about to plan some party. I don't do that shit, I just go to parties."

"Duh, stupid! That's why we hire a party planner! With all the money you make, we can afford a really good one and she can hook our shit up! I think it's a really good idea," I replied.

Dante asked, "Why would we throw this party again?"

"Because," I began, "reason number one, it's a nice way to throw a party that we know won't get shot up—"

"We don't know that for sure," Dante blurted out.

"That's exactly why you get security, baby. Number two, everyone loves a good party. And since this will be one of the hottest events ever, and our name is on it, that automatically boosts your popularity in these streets."

"Yeah, just what I need," he said sarcastically.

"So you're not feeling my idea?"

"You really want to have this party, don't you?" he asked, grabbing me in a hug.

"Hell yeah," I said, caressing his shoulders. "Within the next four to five months. That way it'll be around the time we are making a year too!"

"Kentia, you're lucky I love you. We'll throw the party. I'll give you the money to hire a good party planner okay. Only the best for us, baby. I want this shit at the hottest club, too. We're getting it all!" Dante said.

Now that's what I want to hear, I thought. I smiled and put a kiss on his lips. "Thank you, baby! I got this shit all under control!" I said. I meant that in a literal sense. I did have this shit in my control, and that's how it had to stay.

With Dante's blessing, I hired a superb party planner named Noni. She had credentials from New York City to Hollywood. She was known for planning elite and extravagant parties that made people leave in awe. Now she was planning one of the hottest events to ever go down amongst people in the hoods of Los Angeles. She had five months to plan one of the biggest parties Southern California had ever seen. We decided on the third Saturday of November for the date of the party.

The Ballers' Party was going down in a club on Sunset Boulevard. With Dante's cash, we could afford for it to be there. Announcements were made on the radio stations Power 106 and 93.5 KDAY to come, for the price of thirty dollars a head. Every hustler and female who received a personal invite was automatically VIP for the night, and wouldn't have to pay to get in. Guests had to be sharp and dressed to impress . . . no exceptions. Security would be strictly enforced, securing the safety and well-being of our hood extravaganza.

Of course with Dante and I being the host and hostess, we had to be the flyyest couple in the joint. We flew to New York City on an early Saturday morning to buy our outfits. Dante purchased a Paul Smith charcoal striped, two-button suit with a fishtail cuff and a gray round-collar shirt from the Paul Smith store on Fifth Avenue. I decided to get a Marc Jacobs lilac halter dress at the store on Bleecker Street.

On Monday evening, we flew back to Los Angeles. We had about five days before the party. Word was out all across South Central Los Angeles. Word had even spread as far as the Bay Area in Northern California. People from the cities of San Francisco, Vallejo, Oakland, Sacramento, Fairfield, and Richmond had heard about what was popping off this Saturday in LA.

The party had everyone anxious, and had me excited as hell. There was no doubt in my mind that this party would be the talk of the city for months to come.

Saturday finally came and everybody who was somebody was getting ready for the night's activities. Dante, Hector, Cynthia, Shanti, Taffy, and I showed up to the party about an hour after it started. We exited the limo in front of the club and walked up to the bouncer. He recognized our faces and let us in with no questions asked. The line to get in was almost around the corner. I knew it was going down tonight. We stepped into the club ready to be seen.

As we made our way to the VIP section, I watched the hoes approach Dante. These women were throwing hugs, cheek kisses, and phony smiles his way. They probably would've thrown their thongs at him if it weren't for being in the club . . . not that that would ever stop some of them.

A girl in a lousy pink minidress pulled his arm from around my waist and wrapped it around hers. "Hey, Dante baby. Where you been at? I've been missing you," she said, now wrapping Dante's arms around her neck.

"I been with my girl," Dante said, pulling away from her. He grabbed my hand and put me face to face with the girl. "Right here, Kentia. Remember the one I told you about?"

She looked me up and down. "Dante, you didn't tell me about this girl." She gave a fake laugh.

"Well, now he just did, didn't he?" I asked with an attitude. *No, this bitch didn't just try to play me and play herself by acting like she ain't heard of me from his mouth*, I thought. *But maybe she really didn't. Maybe Dante is just trying to cover up because his side-flings are in the club.*

The bitch rolled her eyes and continued on with Dante. "So, are we going to hook up later on tonight?" she asked.

Dante looked at me, looked at her, and shook his head. "Sorry, Felicia. It ain't going down like that," he said.

"EVER!" I added sarcastically. I smiled at her to show her I had the upper hand, and I loved it.

"You know he's just saying that 'cuz you around here. If it was just me and him it would be another story," Felicia said, rolling her eyes and rolling her neck.

I believed her, but I couldn't let her know that . . . nor could I let Dante know that. "But it ain't just you and him, now is it? It's me and him. Now usually I would sit and argue with your ho ass, but tonight I look flyy and I ain't tryin'a let no silly bitch like you fuck my night up. So, hate on, homegirl, but tonight it's about Dante and me. Better luck next time," I said, grabbing Dante and walking away.

"Believe dat, *beeyotch*!" Shanti yelled at her for emphasis. She laughed with Cynthia as we walked away.

I wondered just how many girls like Felicia were in the club, and how many of them messed with Dante on the side. When it came down to it, I looked like the fool because he was fucking them on the side of our relationship anyway. No matter how bad I cursed them out or how evilly I stared, these hoes still had a piece of him. After tonight, I could get rid of Dante and the ho baggage that came with him. I would have a list of other top-flight dudes to victimize. Dante would be a thing of the past.

After chilling out in VIP, I felt like getting my dance on. I grabbed Shanti and Cynthia and led them to the dance floor. "C'mon, girl! Let's go dance! It's some cuties getting their dance on," I said as we walked down the stairs and onto the dance floor.

We parted through the crowd to the center of the dance floor. You could tell who was from Southern California and who was from Northern California. The Southern Cali boys from the cities of LA, Watts, Inglewood, Compton, and Long Beach were more laid-back and low-key. The Northern Cali boys were flamboyant in their bright colored outfits, platinum jewelry, and grills to match. They were all about having a good time, which attracted me to dance with them.

The DJ spun into the latest party song, and I grabbed one of the Northern California boys and danced with him. His boys followed suit and started dancing with Cynthia and Shanti. After we danced till we couldn't dance any more, we went to the restroom to see the state of our beauty.

I looked in the mirror to make sure my hair was still on point and makeup was still looking fresh. I didn't sweat my hair out too bad, and my makeup was in order. Shanti, on the other hand, had loosened up the curls in her hair. She tried her best to salvage them and made it work for her. Cynthia's hair was fine. She still felt it necessary to put some water on her hand and slick her edges back, which she could do because she was blessed with good hair.

The three of us went back up to VIP. We were ready for mingling. Cynthia was on her best behavior because Hector wasn't having that. He was nice enough to let her dance tonight. Shanti was the free social chick and flirted with every guy who smelled good. However, she took into consideration that there were some guys I wanted and she left them alone. I had to be sneaky because these fellas knew I was on Dante's right arm tonight. They also saw the hoes sweating him and figured out that everything wasn't all that it appeared to be. Boy, were these hustlers grimey! They willingly gave me their number. Two of them even offered to let me come to their hotel after the club.

I had to decline because this was my last night of sleeping with Dante, and tomorrow would be my last day of draining what I could from his wallet.

The party ended at four in the morning. Everyone left satisfied and worn out. We had danced our shoes off and partied ourselves tired. Now it was time for everyone to go to their homes or hotel rooms and sleep themselves sober.

Dante and I went to our hotel room and made some bed-rocking love. He put it down on me so damn good, it seemed as if he knew I was leaving and this was his plea for me to stay. But boredom was the key element in our relationship, and I couldn't take that. He had bought my love, and now it was getting repossessed.

Moving Right Along

Breaking up with Dante the following night only prepared me to mess with his hustling homies. After we woke up that morning, we took a nice warm shower together and got ready for the rest of the day. After checking out of the hotel, Dante took me to Melrose Avenue to shop. I splurged what I could, using the cash out of his wallet. The lovemaking we did the night before came into play, because on this day he was very generous.

Before dropping me off at home, I told Dante to take me to his house. He willingly did so, believing that it was time to get some pussy again. When we got into the house, I asked to see his phone because mine was not working. Dante gave me his phone, not knowing that my phone was perfectly fine and this was all part of my devious plan. After making my phony phone call, I began browsing through the pictures in Dante's phone.

After seeing about fifteen pictures of me, six of him, and three of his little nephew, I came across a nude picture of Felicia, the girl from the club. I complained, and secretly held in the excitement I was getting from finally being able to end this thing . . . legitimately. I got really pissed off when Dante treated the subject so nonchalantly and acted as if it was no big deal. I demanded he take me home, and he did so with no questions asked.

This was just fine with me because I had connected with one of his friends last night. His name was Raymond. Although he was only one of the seven guys whose numbers I had gotten last night, he and I connected the most. His outward appearance was somewhat a disguise. While everyone seemed to overdo it with flashy suits and fedoras and canes, he was low-key, in cream-colored slacks and blue gators with a matching blue belt, also gator skin. His features were to die for! With a handsome face, football-player build and creamy brown skin, I couldn't pass him up.

The conversation began casually. He knew I was Dante's girl, but still decided to talk to me. I was nervous about him at first because he seemed like a good guy that obeyed the rule: "Bros over hoes." Because he offered me his number before I could ask, I knew it was safe to make further moves. I wasn't going to end things with Dante until I was secure about the future.

So just like that, Dante was a thing of the past.

On to Raymond

My new man was a Crip named Raymond. He stayed on LaSalle and Thirty-ninth, making him one of 30s Crips' very own and an OG from the clique, 2Nasty Crips. He was doing big things in his hood. Raymond owned a chop shop and was known for being the best chop shop go-to guy around. When it came to cars, every thug went to him for business. Everyone answered to him, but he answered to me.

We immediately hit it off from the first phone conversation we had. A week after the party, he called me. I immediately told him how fine I thought he was and how on looks alone I wanted to be with him. I catered to his ego and that turned him on. He asked me if we could become an item. I was hungry for the transition and I jumped on the opportunity. Just like that, Raymond became my man. Every other night I was at his house sexing him crazy. He would bless me with at least two hundred when I did a good job, which I always did. This was a minor upgrade from Dante. Dante gave gifts, and Raymond gave money. This was what I wanted.

Raymond and I were riding down King Boulevard toward Manual Arts High School in his royal blue Dodge Charger. He had to pick up his younger brother, Rodney, from school. This would be my first time meeting Rodney. I had seen him in Raymond's pictures before, but never in person. From what Raymond told me, Rodney was a fifteen-year-old terror following in his footsteps.

Raymond pulled up in front of the high school's front entry. We waited a good ten minutes before Rodney came running toward the car. He flung the door open and damn near jumped into the back seat.

"Go, nigga, go!" he yelled.

Raymond sped off. I made eye contact with him. We both were wondering what the hell was going on. Rodney was cracking up with laughter, holding his stomach and stomping his foot onto the car floor.

"Ay yo, what the hell happened?" Raymond asked.

Rodney answered, "Me and the rest of 2Nasty jumped this punk-ass Mexican. We beat his Spanish-speaking ass! Then Li'l Loc took his pistol out and *whop, whop, whop*! Homie went upside his head about three good times!"

I gave Raymond the eye. "Wow," I mouthed the words.

"Y'all young 2Nasty niggas are a trip," Raymond replied. "Where my money at?"

Rodney dug in his pocket and took out a wad of cash trapped in a rubber band. "Let me hold two hunnit," Rodney said, taking out two hundred dollars from the wad.

"Give me the rest, you li'l buster," Raymond said, snatching the rest of the money from his brother.

I held my hand out. Raymond sucked his teeth and gave me a twenty. "What I'ma do with a dub?" I asked, turning my nose up at the twenty resting in my hand.

"Hold it," Raymond answered sarcastically.

"And who is this?" Rodney asked, referring to me.

"Kentia, my girl," Raymond answered.

"Where you snatch this one at?" Rodney asked. "She looks hella better than the last two put together. You got a little sister?"

I laughed. "No, sorry."

Raymond almost seemed embarrassed by Rodney. He changed the subject. "You talk to Daddy?"

Rodney sucked his teeth and replied, "Is that even a real question? Rafael doesn't even call his own mother. What make you think he's gonna call his badass son that he don't even claim?"

Rafael, Raymond and Rodney's father, was doing time for attempted murder. He'd tried to kill their meth-addicted mother, Recita, when he caught her prostituting herself underneath the Harbor Freeway on Slauson Avenue late one Tuesday night. She was trying to make some money to buy some meth from her dealer located in Huntington Park. She had already managed to sell almost everything in her household, from televisions to a bookshelf, over the course of four months. In the last of those four months, Raymond and Rodney's grandmother took the two boys under her wing and moved them in with her. They watched Recita destroy her life.

Recita finally grew up and checked herself into rehab, where she was still at to this day.

Raymond just shook his head slowly. He made a turn onto Normandie. When we reached his grandmother's house on Forty-first Street, Rodney hopped out of the car as quickly as he hopped in. "Good looking out, Ray. I'll holla at you later, cuz," Rodney said, closing the car door.

Raymond pulled off and shook his head. "That's Rodney for you . . . on his way to ghetto superstardom."

"Like you?" I asked.

Raymond nodded his head. "Yeah, like me. You hungry, Kentia?"

"Starving," I told him.

Raymond went to the Burger King on Western Avenue and King Boulevard. He ordered us two number ones at the drive-through, and we drove to his house to eat.

Once parked in front of his home, I knew what would happen for the rest of the day. I would wait for Raymond to get through playing his Xbox 360, then we would fuck the hell out of each other, and I'd get paid and then dropped off at home. It was so much of the same old routine, it was almost boring.

Raymond surprised me when he said, "Is it okay if I call my homie Justice to come through to play the Xbox?"

I shrugged my shoulders and answered, "I don't care. He's your friend."

Raymond did indeed call his boy Justice, who was far better-looking than him.

He stepped out of his ride and came into my view.

Where was he at the Ballers' Party? I thought, as I watched him from the window. "Your friend is here," I told Raymond.

Raymond didn't respond.

Justice just walked right in. I looked at his sexy ass as he entered the room. He was six foot one, about one shade under light skin, sporting nice gear and an even fade.

"Nigga, you shouldn't just leave your doors open. It ain't safe," Justice said as he made himself welcome.

"Fuck dat! That's you! I tell you, man, y'all Hoover niggas are too uptight," Raymond said, rolling a thick blunt that I personally wanted to take a hit of.

"And that's why y'all thirties Crips are dropping like flies," Justice replied, sitting down next to him on the couch. "Y'all just might be the wackest Crips on this side of LA."

"Don't disrespect the hood, cuz," Raymond said playfully, but meaning every word.

"C'mon, man, hook this shit up. I'm 'bout to whup that ass in Madden," Justice replied.

Raymond accepted the challenge and set up the Xbox. "Kentia, go find something to do. You don't want to watch us men play this."

"Don't worry, I can handle," I replied. *And I'll watch your friend*, I thought. "I won't bug, Raymond."

Raymond let me stay and watch them play Madden. I was really eyeing Justice, who occasionally gave me the eye every now and then. I knew we were making some kind of connection.

Opportunity arose when Raymond went to the bathroom. The conversation was quick, but I got what I needed.

"How long you been knowing Raymond?" I asked.

"Since this past June," Justice answered. "How long y'all been an item?"

"Like a month," I answered. "But I'm tryin'a move on to better things."

"Ah, for real?" he asked. He nodded his head as if he was that better thing.

"Like you."

"Say what?"

"I said, like you," I repeated. "You ain't got to worry about making Raymond mad, cuz we ain't 'bout to be no item no more."

With that being said, Justice took out his phone. "What's your number? If you're lucky, I might call."

I fed him my number. I added, "Yeah, you better call if you want all this." I stood up and walked in front of him, giving him a good glimpse of my rear.

"You a trip." He grinned, and I knew I had him right then and there.

That night after Justice left, Raymond and I had rough sex. He broke me off with my cash and took me home. The next night it happened again, and again on the following night.

Over the course of the next two weeks, I grew extremely bored with Raymond. I started feeling like a prostitute more than a gold digger, and I had Justice telling me to be on his team. The boredom

I had felt with Dante began to arise in my relationship with Raymond. Therefore, I started growing
closer to Justice, who'd proved early on he was
the one to be with.

While I was still with Raymond, Justice purchased a Tiffany & Co. silver jewelry set complete
with a charm bracelet, a necklace, a ring and earrings. The amount was unknown, but when I did
my search on online, it accumulated to over eight
hundred dollars.

After a month and two weeks of being with Raymond, I broke things off with him and moved on
to what seemed like better.

Know Justice,

No Peace

I don't know what it was with the Crips, but I was drawn to them like a magnet. Justice seemed to be a financial double threat. He spent cash and gave cash. That's what I liked most about him. Every other day I was given luxurious gifts, and on the days in between, I was handed cash.

But there was a dark side to the drug kingpin from Hoover Crip. I tried to ignore it, but it kept brewing up drama every chance it could. The incident occurred when Corey and I went to the South Bay Galleria to buy Gertrude a gift for her birthday.

We were just strolling past the movies when Justice came out of the cut and started yelling at us.

"Kentia! Bitch, who the fuck is this?" Justice asked, grabbing my wrist.

"Chill, Justice, chill out!" I whined, trying to break loose and calm him down at the same time. *What a coincidence! The day I take my ass to*

South Bay is the same day Justice is up here, I thought.

"Hey, homie, don't grab my little sister like that," Corey said in my defense.

"Don't tell me what to do with my bitch," Justice said. "Who the fuck are you?" Justice was still holding onto my wrist violently as he got in Corey's face, ready to brawl.

"Justice, that's my god-brother!" I yelled.

Justice pushed me away. "That nigga can talk right? RIGHT?"

I nodded my head and looked at Corey.

Justice continued, "Can't you talk, muthafucka?"

Corey looked Justice up and down slowly, cocked his head to the side, and blew an angry breath of wind. "Man, chill the fuck out. I *am* her god-brother," he answered.

Justice looked at me and told me to come over to him. Slowly, I made my way over to him. He wrapped his arm around my neck and apologized. "All right, Kentia, I'm sorry about this whole thing, okay? I just don't like seeing you with other niggas. You know I want you to be my girl, and my girl only. You forgive me, baby?" He added a kiss to my forehead.

I nodded my head and said, "Yeah, I forgive you."

"Good girl. All right, look, here's some money for you to spend, okay?" Justice took out his wallet and gave me almost five hundred dollars. "I love you, girl."

"I love you too, boo," I said, giving him a kiss.

Justice went back over to his boys and let Corey and I continue on our way.

Corey was shocked. He began, "So it's like that, huh? It's that easy for you to just let that nigga slide?"

"Relax, Corey, I know what I'm doing," I said. I truly did know what I was doing. Justice just had a jealous streak that I could easily calm when using the right words.

"That nigga is crazy," Corey warned.

"But he ain't gon' do shit. He just be acting like that to scare me, and please believe, ain't nobody scared of his ass!" I laughed.

"Yeah, right. The first time he put his hands on you, you know who to call. I'll be there in a minute to whup his ol' crazy ass!"

"Yeah, you can't challenge his ass to a game of football, Corey." I laughed.

"I'm serious, Kentia. Where are you picking these clowns up?" he asked angrily. Corey sucked his teeth as he thought about what just happened.

"He's not that bad. He just didn't know who you were," I said, making up an excuse for Justice. I just wanted Corey to shut his mouth about my relationship when he knew nothing about it.

After the mall incident, Justice became strict on me, and even stricter on the cash. Steadily, the money I used to be given was being held back. The luxurious gifts even came to a halt. I'd be better off single and selling jewelry, now that Justice had stopped giving me what I desired.

Justice came and picked me up one night from my house. We were supposed to be going out to dinner and a movie.

I told Gertrude I'd be home before two in the morning, my set curfew—not that I came in at that hour. She just nodded her head sternly, knowing that I wouldn't be home by two. I looked into her eyes and saw anguish that I knew I was the cause of. She wanted to speak up on my recent behavior, but kept silent about it. That was the right mindset because I was not in the mood to be bothered with what was upsetting her.

I got into Justice's car and read the angry look on his face.

"What's wrong, baby?" I asked. "It's a Friday night, and we're about to have a nice time. Why you mugging me so damn hard?"

"My nigga said he saw you walking down Vernon with some dude. What the fuck is that about?" Justice asked.

Yeah, I was walking with another dude. Why the hell you got your boys scoping me out, you insecure asshole! "Are you sure it was me?" I said, trying to put on the "confused" game.

"Don't sit up here and try to play me. The homie said you had on a pink jumpsuit, the same one I got you from Vegas. Who the fuck was you walking with?" Justice asked, screeching away from the curb. He was driving extremely fast, and it was starting to scare me.

"Slow down, Justice!" I exclaimed. "Why you driving like a damn fool?"

"Answer my question!"

"It was my friend, baby."

"What's his name? And don't lie to me!"

"His name is Jeremy," I said, leaning my head on the window.

Justice just nodded his head. There was a mute moment in the car.

"Where does he stay at?' he asked after two minutes of silence.

"On Tenth Avenue," I said, ready to cry. Justice had really pissed me off. "Don't do anything to him. It wasn't his fault. He didn't do anything. Nigga, if you got a problem then take it out on me!"

"Ain't you a brave bitch?" Justice chuckled. "I'ma fix you, though. It's all good. Don't trip."

Justice threatened to "fix me" the whole ride to his house.

"I thought we were going out to eat," I said as I got out of the car, flummoxed about going to his house. I secretly prayed to God that there was somebody else home, just in case he tried to hurt me.

"Just shut the fuck up," Justice said. He grabbed me violently and took me into the house. We argued down the hall toward the back of his house, where his room was.

I decided to call a truce with him and apologize. I apologized over and over again as I watched him down a bottle of vodka.

He then took my hair into his hands, pulled my head back and said, "Don't ever let me or my boys catch you with another nigga again. You understand me?"

"Uh-huh," I moaned.

He roughly slapped a kiss on me. I was confused, but didn't feel like asking any questions as he fiercely unfastened my pants and unbuttoned my shirt. He tossed me on the bed like a rag doll and climbed on top of me. Then, he turned me over and proceeded to have sex with me against my will.

I begged him to stop repeated times.

"Nah, I ain't gon' stop!" he ranted. "You gon' take this shit right here! I bet you won't be seeing a nigga behind my back no more! Shit about to change now! You ain't gettin' shit from me! You got that, bitch?"

I cried for the first time in a long time over a man. It wasn't even because he hurt me emotionally, he was hurting me physically.

When he finally came and pulled out of me, I collapsed on the bed and rolled onto the floor. My stomach hurt like hell and was already cramping up. I went to the bathroom and threw up in the toilet. Justice didn't even enter the bathroom to see if I was okay.

The next weekend I was turning nineteen. I already knew I was going to wish for the best man to date. This guy would have to go above and beyond for me and give me everything I wanted when I wanted it. He would have to be the cream of the crop. And I vowed to drain that nigga for everything he had!

I moved to plan two of the Justice Case. Any chance I had to get to his stash while alone in his house, I took my share. Justice would accuse his little thug sister of stealing his money, assuming I didn't know where he kept his stash. He would then go upside her head with a quick slap. Personally, I didn't care, as long as I had my hundreds by the end of the week. Stealing from the stashes seemed to be very easy for me.

In the meantime, I worked on a new relationship with a man named Lamont, who had the potential to make my birthday wish come true. Lamont and I met at Venice Beach on a Sunday afternoon. He was walking his dog, and I was going to the beach with Shanti. I was attracted to his bold appearance and clean-cut style. I bravely made the first move of introducing myself. During what I knew would be my last days with Justice, I began to build my relationship with him.

One grave Friday night, Justice caught me stealing red-handed and slapped my face red. He told me not to do it again and left it at that. Don't no man put his hands on me in that manner; therefore I got the hell out Dodge and left him for good.

Lust, Love, and Lamont

Lamont was the oldest guy I had talked to, making him a puzzling twenty-nine. I wasn't sure if he would be down for talking to this fresh nineteen-year-old. Lamont only found that even sweeter, claiming I was innocent. He must've thought I was inexperienced. I was ready to work this man and everything he had. He wasn't my average type. He wasn't a drug dealer or an illegal worker. He had a legit job at a company in Culver City and was very well off for his age. I wondered why he was still single and not yet married.

Lamont was the ultimate sugar daddy. He was—almost—good in bed, good in giving me cash, and good with his expenses. He did the whole nine. I actually felt like I was in an honest relationship with him.

We had been going together for almost a year, which was a record, because I never planned on staying with him that long. I didn't even talk to other guys while with Lamont because he gave me everything I needed. Lamont fulfilled the first part of my birthday wish, but the vow I made to myself about draining him for everything had to be put on hold. He was kind and respectful toward me, and that threw me out of my element. I wasn't ready to leave him just yet. I had fallen in love with him.

This particular Monday morning, he had a surprise for me. I had caught the bus to his house on Sunlight Place near Baldwin Hills Recreation Center.

He let me into his lovely home. "Hey, Kentia. How you doing?" he asked, putting on a tie.

"Where are we going, and why you dressed in Sunday's best? I thought you didn't have to work," I said, hoping he saw that I was dressed in a girly sweat suit.

Lamont chuckled and replied, "No, they called me in this morning. I am taking you to the DMV to take your test to get your license."

I panicked. "WHAT THE HELL IS WRONG WITH YOU?"

"Relax, Kentia. You can't hold onto your permit forever. You need to get your license. You need a new sense of independence. I know you'll pass. You're a good driver. You think I would let you drive my car if I thought you couldn't drive? And don't I have a nice car?"

"Yes, you do," I said, a picture of Lamont's red Ferrari popping into my head.

"Do you have your permit and social security card?" he asked as he slipped into his dressy Stacy Adams.

"I have my permit, but my social is at home," I answered. "I can't believe you scheduled a test for me. Oh my goodness, Lamont. I could slap you silly right now."

I followed him out the back door, which led into the garage. He opened the garage door with the push of a button and proceeded to get into the driver's side of the Ferrari. I got into the passenger side.

After starting up the car, he backed out of the driveway and pulled out into the street. Lamont took me back to my house and waited out front as I went in to retrieve my social.

Gertrude was on the sofa, watching her favorite soap opera.

"Hey God-Mommy! I might get my license today. Hopefully I pass!" I told her, excitement obvious in my tone.

"Who is taking you? Lamont?" Gertrude asked.

How does she know? I never even told her about Lamont, I thought. "Um, yeah, how did you know?"

"The question is why haven't you told me?" Gertrude asked. "Corey told me about this man. He's twenty-nine?"

"Yes. I'm nineteen. So what's the problem?" I asked her.

Gertrude groaned uneasily and replied, "I usually keep quiet about what's going on with you. But, as your godmother and your guardian, I feel I have the right to talk to you about what I feel."

Now you want to act like you care, I thought as I rolled my eyes.

"Now you know your curfew is two AM. Sometimes you never come home," Gertrude said.

"I be at Shanti's."

"And if that's the case, you are supposed to call me," Gertrude responded.

"Well, it's early in the morning and I don't want to wake you up."

"Kentia, I ain't no damn fool. If you know you're not going to come home, don't tell me you are when you leave my house. I'm going to be strict on the rules. If you can't come home by two in the morning, don't come home at all. You can go live with Shanti, if that's the case, or live with this Lamont twenty-nine-year-old character," Gertrude said firmly.

I knew she meant every word she said. If it was that easy, I could live with Shanti, but that wasn't what I wanted to do. Lamont and I, even with our beautiful and healthy relationship, were not ready to live together. So I knew I had to take responsibility for my actions and apologize.

"All right, God-Mommy. I am very sorry I haven't been respecting the house rules. But I will start respecting them," I answered out of obligation.

Gertrude nodded and told me I could go on doing what I had to do.

I went into the bedroom, found my social security card, and left the house.

Lamont took me to the Inglewood DMV and told me what to do. I was to go into the DMV, sign in for my test that Lamont registered me for, and wait for my number to be called.

I followed his exact orders. Next thing I knew, I was in the testing car taking my driving test.

We got back on Manchester, made a right on Eucalyptus, and cruised down Queen Street. She directed me back to the DMV. I had passed. It was not as stressful as I thought it would be. I probably caught her on a good day.

We went inside the DMV, and they issued me my license, saying I should receive the hard copy in about a week.

I called Lamont's cell phone and told him the good news.

"See, baby? I knew you would pass," he said proudly. "I'm on the way right now, okay?"

"Okay," I chimed.

I waited patiently for him at the DMV. He sent me a text message when he was parked outside.

I left the DMV with a smile on my face. I was glad that Lamont cared so much about me that he would help me get my license.

"All right, now that you got your license, it's time for step two," Lamont said.

"What's step two?" I asked.

"Buying you a car," he replied.

"WHAT?" I squealed. "Lamont, don't fuck with me!"

"I'm not! Seriously, I have a friend who owns a *slightly* used car dealership, and plans to hook me up with a nice ride at a nice price," Lamont replied as we headed for the city of Hawthorne.

"Oh my goodness! Are you for real? Lamont, ooh, if we weren't driving I'd give you some pussy!" I joked.

Lamont laughed and cranked up the radio. "Let's celebrate," he said as he put on "Celebration" by Kool and The Gang.

I laughed at his music selection as I snapped my fingers rhythmically.

This seemed too perfect. The day I got my license would be the same day I got a car. "So why are you getting me a car anyway?"

"'Cuz I got the money," Lamont bragged. "No, I'm just kidding."

I knew part of him wasn't kidding.

"I'm getting you a car because, number one, you need it. Number two, I'm trying to help you get on your feet. You're almost twenty and you should have shit like this rolling for you already."

Oh, you are helping me in more ways than you can imagine, I thought as he continued on.

"Do you know how old I was when I first got my car? I was sixteen, and I bought it myself. I worked really hard to get the things I wanted. I know it may be different with you because I'm buying you everything, but you deserve it. You've been such a good girlfriend. I love you, Kentia. And don't forget that," Lamont said.

"I love you too, baby."

When we reached the car dealership, Lamont took me straight inside the building to see his friend, Anthony.

Anthony was a conservative and well-educated man who had lots of dough. He greeted Lamont with a firm handshake and a warm grin. "How are you doing, Lamont?" Anthony asked.

"I'm great. Anthony, this is Kentia, my lovely girlfriend. Kentia, this is my good friend Anthony," Lamont introduced us.

I shook Anthony's hand. I had enough small talk already. I wanted to see my car.

"So are we good on the price for the car?" Lamont asked as he followed Anthony out to the lot.

"Yeah, I'm letting it go for thirteen, nine. It's a two thousand one model. You have a forty-two thousand mileage and automatic transmission. I hope she likes the color silver because that's what color it is, and the inside is black leather. Four doors, AM/FM, CD system, and some nice ten-inch rims," Anthony described, leading us past the different cars.

He would say everything about the car, except what it is, I thought impatiently as I followed close behind. "What kind of car is it?" I asked.

"Voilà!" Anthony said, stretching his hand toward a silver Lexus ES 300.

"I LOVE IT!" I said, picturing myself driving down Crenshaw Boulevard in the ride that was a check away from being mine.

"We'll take it," Lamont said. "Now, listen, Kentia. I'm going to buy the car, so you won't have to make any payments. You are going to have to get insurance and pay for that. Can you do that?"

"Yes, yes, I can!" I said anxiously, waiting to get in the car.

That day I drove off the lot in my new ride. Lamont was right behind me in his Ferrari. How in the world did I luck up with him? I could not leave a man like this. The relationship was genuine, financially secure, and most importantly, it was real. I wasn't faking it with Lamont. I had truly fallen for him. I was going to keep the fire burning as long as I could.

Lamont and I returned to the house. I parked my car in front of the house, and he parked his in the garage. We entered the house and went straight into the kitchen. I scanned through the refrigerator to see what there was to eat.

He went to the phone and saw there was a new message. On speaker, he listened to the message.

"You have one new message. First message: Lamont, it's Shelly. I don' t mean to bother you, but it's urgent. Your daughter and I don't have any money. I don't think it's fair that you can wine and dine this young girl but you can't even get your daughter a fuckin' gift for her birth—"

Lamont immediately deleted the message, hoping I didn't hear as much as I did. I turned around abruptly and walked toward him. "Excuse me?"

Lamont was sweating bullets. His face was red with embarrassment. "Kentia, baby I—"

"No, no, no, no," I said, shaking my head. I didn't want to believe what I had just heard, but I did. "Are you serious? Why didn't you tell me you had a baby?"

"It isn't easy to tell the one you love that you have a baby with a girl you never wanted to be with," Lamont answered.

"Well, it's much harder to tell the one you love when you are deep into the relationship," *I* answered. "Start explaining."

"Shelly and I had a relationship over a year ago, before I met you. Three months into the relationship, I realized I didn't want to be with her. So we broke up, but three weeks later she found out she was pregnant," Lamont explained.

"Then what did you do?" I asked, noticing he stopped as if that was all there was to say.

"I told her I wanted a DNA test when the baby

was born. I was there at the delivery, saw her give birth, and I cut the umbilical cord," Lamont said.

"And you were the father?"

"Ninety-nine-point-nine percent."

I sighed and shook my head as I held back the tears that were aching to come down. "Lamont? Why didn't you just tell me? I would've been able to accept it," I said, not really sure if I would have.

"I don't know why I didn't tell you," Lamont answered. "Honestly, I don't know."

It hurt like hell to know that I had to break things off with Lamont for the time being. He had bigger things to worry about than me. He had a baby who needed his attention, affection, and love. Instead, he was giving all that to me, and that was wrong. I let him know how I felt.

"Lamont, maybe we should just chill out on each other for a while," I said solemnly.

"Kentia, no!" Lamont pleaded. "Don't let this be the end of us."

"It isn't the end, it's just a long pause. You should really be involved in your child's life. I mean, I grew up fatherless, so I know how it feels. Don't let that baby suffer for what you consider your mistake," I said.

"You're right," Lamont answered.

I knew I was right. That was obvious. I didn't want to leave Lamont, but I had to. The first time I ever felt sincere about a guy was a failure . . . and here came that futile thinking.

All my relationship projects are incapable of producing definite results. It's ineffective to love. I should've stuck to the original plan . . . simply gold digging.

The more I stayed around and thought about it, the angrier I got. "Do I still get to keep the car?" I asked.

"Aw, c'mon, babe. Of course you do! I'm not that shallow," Lamont said with an endearing smile.

"All right, I'll keep in touch," I said, not sure if that was true. "I should go."

"I love you, Kentia," he said, before I could touch the doorknob to the front door.

I turned around, looked at him, and fixed my lips to say the same. "I love you, Lamont," I answered, surprised I was able to say that. "You're one of a kind."

And in my book, he really was. For the first time I did not want to leave a man, but I was forced to.

Omar the Great

"C'mon, Shanti! You gon' make us miss the action, with your ass taking so damn long!" I said, eagerly waiting on her couch as she got dressed in her room.

"Nope, this is payback for all the times you made me wait when we were about to go somewhere! Now that you driving you think I'm going to show you some mercy? Hell to the nah!" Shanti yelled.

I rolled my eyes and played a game on my cell phone as she finished her business.

She came out in some Seven jeans, black boots, and a black halter top. "Do I look flyy or what?"

"You look decent," I answered. "But you shoulda stepped your game up." I got up and twirled around in my Prada short set. "Now, this is flyy."

Shanti sucked her teeth. "Whatever, girl. Let's go," Shanti said as she walked toward the front door.

I followed her out and went toward my car.

Shanti was excited about my new ride, almost more excited than me.

"Oh, bitch, this is hot! I like this shit! Lamont paid this off all the way?" Shanti asked, walking around the Lexus.

"Hell yeah, all the way! I just pay the insurance, and that's still his money!" I giggled as I unlocked the doors.

Shanti and I got in the car. She said, "So what you gon' do when you quit his ass?" She moved the seat back and made herself comfortable.

"Get the money from the next victim," I said. "And I'm going to find his ass tonight on the boulevard!"

"Go 'head, bitch! Go 'head!" Shanti cheered me on.

I started the car, turned up the radio, and hit Crenshaw from Shanti's house. We went a little past Vernon and made a U-turn to get on the other side of Crenshaw. We drove up near El Pollo Loco, where the pimped-out rides were posted up. It was like a giant car show, except nobody was sitting around explaining what they did to their car. Everyone was socializing, having a good ol' gangsta time . . . before the police came and swept everybody up out of there.

It always happened on a Sunday evening. This was the place to be. Shanti and I mingled with all the other females who were either the girlfriend of a baller, the ho of a pimp, or another gold digger looking for her way into the pockets of a hustler. Some of these bitches were banging their hoods harder than the guys. Not Shanti and I. We were one of the flyy girls showing off tonight.

We talked to some of the other girls, ones we knew and ones we'd just met. I hugged some of the guys I went to school with. Shanti had gotten lost in the crowd as she walked around with her ex-boyfriend, Isaiah. I kept stunting solo, and eventually found the man I wanted to be my next victim.

I walked over to the swarthy gentleman sitting on the hood of his '64 Impala with green candy paint and twenty-four-inch rims. I had me a winner. I casually walked up and started a cool conversation.

"This is a nice ride you got here," I said, running my fingers across the top of the Impala.

"Yeah," he said nonchalantly. His eyes looked me up and down. He hopped off the hood of the car.

"You must like for your rides to sit high, 'cuz these rims you got are real nice. I wonder how much this cost you," I said, eyeing the car one more time before I laid eyes on him.

"A grip," he replied. "What's your name, li'l mama?"

"Kentia. What's your name?"

"Omar," he replied hesitantly.

Omar, I thought. There was only one Omar who was known in these streets. He was Omar the Great, running the biggest Los Angeles drug empire of today. I had heard of him, and wanted him since hearing of his street cred. Tricking the police and beating the feds, so many people wondered how Omar was doing his thing. If I could get my hands on him, I'd be the top bitch in the LA. That's the kind of shit I wanted. From that moment on, Omar was mine.

"Where you from, Omar?" I asked, moving in closer to him. I made sure to put my hands on my hip and poke my breasts out a little bit.

"Are you tryin'a bang on me? Don't worry 'bout where I'm from. Shit, where you from?" he asked.

"I don't bang, homie," I said. "I'm a lady."

"And females who are in gangs ain't ladies?"

"I ain't said that, but it sure does take away from their femininity. Don't you think so?" I asked. "Who would you rather get with? A female who is too thugged-out for her own good? Or a smooth, model-figure flyy girl who got that sex appeal?"

"I like the second one," Omar answered. "Am I talking to one of those right now?"

I laughed. "You know you are. Don't even try to play dumb like that. So when can I get your number, Omar?"

"Take my shit down right now," Omar said.

I took out my phone and handed it to him. "You put it in there yourself. Give me your phone and let me put my number in there," I said sticking my hand out. He put his Blackberry phone in my hand. I entered my number into his phone and handed it back to him.

In return, he handed me mine. "So when you gon' call me?" Omar asked, opening his car door.

"Whenever you want me to," I replied. "When are you available?"

"Call me whenever. My phone is always on," Omar said, getting into the driver's seat. "What are you doing after this?"

"Me and my girl Shanti will probably just ride

out somewhere. Maybe to the beach or something. Why? What are you doing?" I asked him, leaning on the door.

"I got to go handle some business. Some business pretty girls like you don't need to get involved with, na'mean?" Omar said. He started the car, and I moved away so he could close the door. After closing the door, he rolled the window down.

"Oh, you right," I replied. "Well, call me when you done handling who or whatever. My phone ain't always on, but if you're lucky it might be."

He just grinned and gave me a casual head nod. After that night, Omar and I started talking. I won him over with my game and charm, and the rest is history, leading up to . . .

Fucking with Omar caused me to return to old habits. Not just gold digging habits, but disrespecting-the-house rules habits. It wasn't like he was Lamont, who was concerned with getting me home on time and actually cared that I could get kicked out if I didn't obey Gertrude's rules. I started coming in later than two AM again, and some nights I didn't come home at all. I didn't care to call and let Gertrude know.

A month into me and Omar's blossoming relationship, Gertrude announced that she could no longer take me disrespecting the house. She told me I had to get out. Shanti had moved her boyfriend into her one-bedroom apartment, and I was not the one to be a third wheel. I didn't even bother to ask her if I could stay with her. When I told Omar the bad news, he turned it into a positive and said I could live with him.

Two months later, I was still holding my place as Omar's number one, and he made sure to make me feel that way.

I had everything at my fingertips, and at Omar's expense. I could bring something I desired to his attention and he would have one of his workers go out and get it for me. This automatically made me feel flyy and in charge. I knew there were females who wanted to be in my position, but I was holding it down so tight, no one could take my spot.

Omar's secret stashes were for my amusement. I would frequently go to his stash and take money from it. He would never notice because all he did was throw stacks of cash in the stash. He was pretty careless about his stash money, which was out of character for a baller, but perfect for the gold digger in me. Omar would have never guessed that I was getting extra money from the stash.

It seemed too good to be true, and three months into the relationship, I found out it was.

On a rainy Thursday afternoon, Omar came into the apartment and went straight to the bedroom. I felt disrespected. I felt I had the given right to receive a "Hello," or some kind of greeting. I cooked, I cleaned, and I did all other things, trying to be the perfect house-girlfriend. The least he could've done was acknowledge me when he came in.

I stopped washing the dishes and followed him into the bedroom. "What's wrong, baby?" I asked.

He shook his head. I could see the anger written all over his face. I was almost afraid to address the situation, in fear of getting yelled at. "Had a bad day?" I asked, sitting down next to him on the bed.

"Obviously," he said sarcastically. He tossed me an irritated look.

I looked away nervously. I got up and started to walk out of the room, but his next question was my hindrance.

"How much fucking money have you been spending, Kentia?" Omar asked.

I shrugged. "I don't know, baby," I answered.

To be honest, within the past week, I had spent over five thousand dollars worth of designer jeans, over seven thousand dollars on five bags, and over ten thousand dollars on some designer shoes. All of this was money from his secret stashes.

"Don't lie to me, bitch. I know you been spending my money," Omar said, getting up off of the bed.

He had never called me *bitch* before, at least not in that manner. "Omar, what are you talking about? Everything I want you give me."

"What about the money I give you?"

"I spend it or save it."

"What about the money in my stash?"

"It should be all there."

"Should be? Should be there? Is it?"

"Yes, Omar, it's there."

"You make me not want to trust you!" he said, storming toward me.

I was getting fearful as he approached me. I refused to go down like a chump. "You better get the fuck out of my face!" I yelled.

Omar looked at me like I was crazy for telling

him what to do. He raised his hand at me. "I oughta slap the shit out of you!"

"You oughta get out of my face!" I said, taking a big risk.

Omar very well could have beaten my ass till I turned purple. Instead, he pushed me down to the floor and told me to get out of the room.

All right then, nigga! You wanna be stupid? Now I'm gon' really spend that cash, I thought as he slammed the bedroom door.

Player versus the Game

On days I knew Omar would be gone for long periods of time, I would hit up the stash, stealing a couple of hundreds for starters. I opened up a bank account and began putting the money in there. I was able to snatch up a total of twenty grand in a month and a half's time. Omar thought he was slick and tried switching up his stash places. But I easily found those too, and took more, just because he wanted to be stupid.

Little did I know, these were Omar's last days to shine, and my spending habits were going to get me in some personal problems.

I had met Cynthia at Roscoe's Chicken and Waffles on Manchester and Main for lunch. I had not spent much time with her since I'd moved in with Omar.

"Damn, *chica*! You're showing!" I said joyfully as I looked at her three months pregnant belly. "Anybody can see that on your tiny self!"

"Girl, I'm trying to hide it. I don't want too many people knowing. How are you and Omar?" she asked.

"Girl, I'm draining this fool's money to the wire. You have no idea. We're at the end of our relationship anyway. It didn't even last as long as I thought it would. I'm even more pissed off that I moved in with this guy," I informed her.

Cynthia shook her head. "You got an account?"

"Yeah, girl, credit or debit! I'm about to be balling all by myself once I'm done with Omar," I bragged as I tossed my hair to the other side of my shoulder.

We laughed and chopped it up nicely. Cynthia gave me all her information about being pregnant, and I gave her my information on being a gold digger.

"Well, let me tell you now, mami," Cynthia began. "If you gon' play Omar, play him slower than normal because the streets are talking, and it's all about him. Word is he's going broke and it ain't because of you. Some guy named Eazy is taking over, and it won't be long until Omar has nothing. And, to add insult to injury, Eazy and his boys been robbing Omar's spots. Omar is about to be broke, *chica!*"

I was shocked. *Omar going broke?* "Hell nah! I got to take everything and leave!" I said. That seemed like a better plan to me.

"No, Kentia. You don't want Omar to know that you were only there for the money. You got to trick him. Just take that shit slowly and act as if nothing is happening," Cynthia suggested. "Girl, he will kill you if you just up and leave his broke ass. And you know he'll find you."

I knew Omar was dangerous before, but now he seemed like a wuss because he was being taken over by Eazy. I was even interested in this Eazy cat. Maybe I could get to him and be his lady. I promised Cynthia I would take things slowly and handle my business.

Over the next few days I tried my best to get whatever cash I could. However, there was little or no cash in there. I realized that Omar had finally gone bankrupt. I was relieved because I was ready to leave his poor ass.

I called Corey and asked him to get a moving van for me. I would stay in Cynthia and Hector's guest house behind their home until I found another place to stay. This Saturday would be my moving day. I could finally get away from Omar and cross him off the list.

He and I had been arguing all week long. When he punched me in my face on Thursday night in a brutal argument, I got my overnight bag and returned to Gertrude's house. I begged her to let me stay for the next couple of days and assured her I would leave on the upcoming Saturday.

Shanti called me on Friday afternoon. I could hear the panic and anger in her voice. I asked her what in the hell was going on.

"I'm 'bout to have Taffy fuck that nigga Omar up!" she screamed into the phone. "Don't nobody pull one over my fucking best friend!"

"Girl, what are you talking about?" I screamed just as loud as her. The anger and panic in her voice almost made me think somebody was dead.

"Kentia, Taffy and his boys just saw Omar on Crenshaw and Slauson selling all these shoes, bags and clothes. He got a big-ass sign that says IT'S REAL! Girl, as soon as he saw Taffy drive by with his middle finger out the window, his ass started packing up. About thirty minutes later when they came back with the rest of the big homies, that nigga was gone! We don't know where he at! They looking for him!" Shanti informed me.

"Aw, shit!" I yelled. "Is he selling my shit?"

"Girl, I think so. Girl, meet me at the apartment. We about to get to the bottom of this bullshit right now!" Shanti instructed. "I'm leaving out the door right now!"

"Meet you there," I said as I fondled around my junky dresser for my car keys. I found them, put on a hoodie, and slipped into some jeans and flip-flops. I left my godmother's house and got in my car, heading for the apartment at full speed.

I was there in seven minutes flat. Shanti was already waiting for me inside her car. She saw me pull up and stepped out of her car. She had a bat in her hand, and her keys interlocked between each finger.

"Girl, he better hope he ain't here 'cuz I'm coming in swinging and leaving out victorious," Shanti forewarned.

We walked up to the door and opened it with my key. Shanti and I raced into the apartment. She had the bat at an angle, as if ready to knock a baseball out of the park. I almost fainted at the sight of the empty apartment. Only a few things were still in their position. I went into the bedroom.

My clothes . . . GONE! My shoes . . . GONE! My purses . . . GONE! My perfumes . . . GONE! My personal belongings . . . GONE! I HAD NOTHING! No furniture, no food, and none of my accessories. There was a note on the ground where the bed used to be. I opened it and read it.

Kentia,
You thought you were the grimiest one, but I got a little dirtier than you. If you didn't know, two can play that game. This is for all the times you stole from me and thought that I didn't know it! Finally, the gold digging bitch has had her day! Don't even try to find me! I'll be long gone by the time you read this! Payback—or nothing back—is a bitch! Ain't it? And so are you!
*   -Omar*

I balled the letter up and tossed it in the air. I didn't shed any tears. He was right, and I deserved everything that had happened to me within the last twenty-four hours. He had beaten me at what I thought was my own game. *Damn*, I thought, *guess I made a bad move.*

I looked at Shanti and found myself back at square one. She looked down in disappointment. I had gone from something to nothing. How could that be? I had everything in order. Shit was supposed to be going my way, and I turned my back on the game for one second and look what happened. I was hoping within the next hour Shanti and I could come up with some brilliant idea that would get me back in the game.

"Well, ain't this a bitch," Shanti said with a fake laugh, hoping she could brighten up the dim situation.

"No, this shit is fucked-up, girl," I replied. "I'm broke as hell with no clothes, no belongings! I ain't got jack! I might as well be homeless."

"C'mon now, Kentia. As pretty as you look, ain't no nigga gon' let you go homeless. What about what's-his- name? The rich dude? Lamont?"

"Girl, please! Lamont got baby mama drama that he needs to work out! And if I call him now after all this time, he'll think I'm using him." I sucked my teeth. I put my hands on my hip and shook my head in disbelief. One day things were all good and gravy and the next they were dreadful.

"What about the cash in your account?"

"Girl, I was spending that!"

"I thought you were saving?"

"Hell, I was saving until Louis Vuitton came out with the fall collection."

I knew Shanti wanted to laugh, but she didn't because she knew I'd be even more pissed. I sighed angrily and said, "Girl, some of my shit still had tags on it. Bitches are going to be on it!"

"Excuse me," said a voice near the entrance of the bedroom. Shanti and I looked toward the door and saw the landlady with some papers in her hand. "Ladies, I need you to leave. I have people coming to look at the apartment."

"What the hell is you talking about? She lives

here," Shanti said pointing to me. "Don't tell us to leave."

I cleared my throat, a way of getting Shanti's ghetto ass to shut the hell up. I walked over to the landlady and said, "Hello, I'm Kentia Bradford. Ma'am, I did used to live here. In fact, the little stuff you see in here is mine."

"Well, the apartment was not in your name, and the person whose name it was in already moved out and informed me. I'm having some men come here to clear this mess out," she replied patiently, even though I knew she was getting fed up with Shanti and me already.

Shanti and I looked at each other and rolled our eyes simultaneously. Shanti held on tight to the strap of her purse and walked toward the bedroom door. I followed her out after giving the landlady an evil glare.

"That shit is ridiculous. You can't even get what's left of your shit out in time," Shanti said, placing her purse on the top of her car.

"Girl, ain't shit in there except old memories. Fuck Omar, fuck his life, and fuck all he stands for . . . which ain't shit!" I said, unlocking the doors to my Lexus.

"I would hate to be in your shoes," Shanti replied.

"Be lucky you're not," I replied. "Where you headed?"

"To Taffy's house to see if they found that nigga Omar before he left town like the bitch he is," Shanti replied. "You gon' follow?"

I shook my head as I opened my car door. "Nope, I'm alright. I'm going to my godmother's house to sleep and find a way out of this shit. I have absolutely nothing left. I lost it all to the hands of some bitch-ass nigga. And, on top of that, bitches gon' be walking around Los Angeles wearing my shit!"

"That's got to be the worst feeling in the world," Shanti said as she got in her car. She started it up. "Holla at me later!" She honked her horn and drove off.

I waved goodbye and proceeded to my car and started it up. I wasn't going to my godmother's house. I just used that as a cover-up so I wouldn't have a reason to go to Taffy's with Shanti.

I tried my best to hold the anger and sadness in, but I couldn't. I buried my face into my hands and cried like an inconsolable baby. Everything I had worked for went down the drain. My schemes and plans became failures because I'd slipped up. It was hard to say, but couldn't be denied. The game beat me. I wasn't playing my best. Now I had to live with my mistakes.

There was a thought in my mind to call Corey and reach out to him. But depending on niggas was what got me here in the first place. I dug this hole, got pushed in it. Now I had to get myself out. I made up my mind. I was not going to call Corey, nor was I going to live with Cynthia. I was going to take my steps, my way, and get the hell on with my life. And, hell nah, I wasn't going back to selling jewelry. That was the old Kentia. I had a new game plan. Sure, the plan I had constructed had flaws, but shit had to be done.

I took out my cell phone and called an old homegirl of mine from the Crenshaw High days.

Her name was Petrona—yes, almost like the drink—but everyone called her Peedi. She was working a late-night job that gave her a cool sum of money.

"Hello?" Peedi answered.

"Hey, Peedi, this is Kentia."

"Hey, Kentia. What up with you, girl? Ooh, I heard you were with Omar? Is that true? And I heard you use to fuck with Dante? What up with that?"

The questions were coming out so fast, but I managed to hear every one.

"Oh, girl, in due time . . . in due time I will tell you all the details. Right now I need you to do me a favor," I said.

"Peedi doing Kentia a favor? Lawd have mercy, what happened?" she asked.

"Nothing, girl! Why you think something happened?" I asked, hoping this wasn't her way of snaking the truth from me when she had already heard a word.

"Sheeit, 'cuz, according to sources, you stay on point, girl. You never need anybody to help you with shit, unless he's a man!" Peedi laughed.

I laughed just to make it seem like I was still at it and doing okay. "Yeah, girl, you know that's how I roll. But I need a side hustle, so it won't look like I'm too lazy," I replied.

"Oh, now that's what I'm talking about! You got game and you running it! Where do I come in into all of this?" Peedi asked.

"All right, I need you to talk to your boss about putting me down for a job," I answered.

"Girl, are you sure you want to do what I do?

Only a few can work it," Peedi replied. "Or you try-in'a go into the other line of work? And even that's hard to do."

"So you tryin'a say I can't do it?" I said, getting an attitude.

"Nah, girl. Never dat." Peedi giggled. "I was being sarcastic. Lighten up. You know I can holla at my ol' man about that."

"Tell him I want housing included," I added.

"Cool," Peedi replied. "I'm about to walk up in there right now. I'll hit you up later on this number, okay?"

"That sounds good. Get at me," I replied before hanging up.

A New Recruit

I walked up the flight of stairs to my new boss's office. A week after the conversation with Peedi, I was finally told to come in and see him. I was glad, because my godmother was getting tired of me being at her house and argued I should have my shit together. But because I had gone through so much, she allowed me extra time. I had applied to numerous clothing stores and was still waiting for a callback. I was broke, something I had to get reacquainted with now that I was out of the "gold-digging-a-man" scene.

I had managed to get some money out of Corey after telling him about my downfall. He willingly took me shopping, knowing it was something I loved to do.

So here I was on my way to my, possibly, new boss's office in some old jeans from Macy's and a halter top from Metropolis in the Fox Hills Mall. My shoes were the sandals I had on my feet the day Omar robbed me.

Peedi greeted me at the door in a bright and

tight orange jumpsuit, looking like a sexy female convict. She winked at me and opened the boss's office. I walked in and sat in front of his desk.

The Boss was a pimp. He had an ongoing pimp-and-ho prostituting and selling goods service that I had decided to stoop to until I had saved enough money to quit. I chose this game because it came with some living arrangements. If hired, I would be living in the "whorehouse" with eight other women who were either selling their bodies or selling drugs. I wanted to sell drugs, not my body. Even though I was in a bad place, I wasn't that bad. I felt I could manage pushing some dope for The Boss.

The meeting was anything but comfortable. I was nervous—I don't know what for—and was eager to know if he was going to put me down or not. With the wink Peedi had given me earlier, I figured I was in. And I was. The Boss put me down as his female pusher, and that was alright with me. I would be rooming with Peedi, who was a prostitute, if you had not guessed yet. She loved doing what she did too. She would parade up and down the streets looking for a man to get on top of. She would find them because she had a banging body and an angelic face.

It seemed like overnight I went from pushing dope at school, to selling jewelry on the streets, to taking the money of the sexiest men in the hoods. Now I was back to square one, pushing dope. I was the living example of one step forward and two steps back. I don't call that progressing; I call it life.

PART TWO:

$$Kirrah Freeman$$

Kirrah Freeman

Amaun and I bobbed our heads to Dre's classic hit "Let Me Ride" as he drove down Manchester. He made a right turn onto Prairie Avenue. There was a block party on Prairie Avenue and 102nd Street. My home girl Nisha was the hostess of this event. She invited her uncle, who worked at the radio station, to come to the block party and broadcast the show from there. Amaun was hoping for a freestyle rap battle. He planned to rip the competition apart with his lyrics. He was a really good rapper too. He performed at Inglewood High School talent shows and threw special performances at our lunch table. I knew his potential and his passion.

We finally made it to the block party. We got out the car and joined in the festivities. Tommy the Clown was there with his famous "Krumpers." They performed and got us all hyped. There was the freestyle battle Amaun had hoped for. Just as I'd predicted, he won the grand prize of three hundred dollars. They had a dancing contest, which I proudly entered. I was one of the last two contestants. We both were so good, they called it a draw because the cheers of the crowd were equally loud for both of us.

My dancing did not go unnoticed. It attracted the attention of a young DJ with the radio station. His name was Mike. We hooked up after the block party and grew to like each other's company. I was already aware of my undeniable beauty, but it was Mike who encouraged me to do something with it. He would often tell me how I looked twice as good as the girls in music videos. He said I could be the next face on a denim ad. He persuaded me to get into modeling.

Mike was my direct connect to success. Surely, if it hadn't been for him, I wouldn't be where I was now. Mike put me down with Carina Sanchez, a personal photographer with a lot of Hollywood credit. She took some amazing pictures of me and secretly submitted them to a local agency.

That was when I got the call from Benny, a twenty-six-year-old agent who believed I had top-notch potential. Mike persuaded me to take a chance with Benny because he seemed like he knew what he was doing, or wanted to do. That's exactly what I did.

Benny was excellent with getting me on photo shoots and positions as an extra in the movies. What Benny had not looked into was music videos, which was what Mike saw me being in.

Mike kept a picture of me hanging from his microphone at the radio station. When the rapper

B-More, Maryland came to the station for an interview, he saw my photo. With much interest, he inquired about me and my whereabouts. Mike told him I was a model and I stayed in Inglewood.

B-More wanted to get me on the set of his video. He pulled some strings with Mike and talked him into getting me to come. Mike hit me up and told me the proposition. Of course I was down for it! I had been waiting to do my first music video ever since I'd started this modeling thing. Benny was all for it, and got me on the set of B-More's video.

I was nervous as hell at the shoot! I just stood by B-More's side and did my little dance when the cameras rolled. I was disappointed with myself after the shoot, and even more devastated when I saw the video on television. I knew I was nervous, but it's so bad when you looked like it. Benny said I looked normal, just like the other girls. But I didn't want to be any other girl. I wanted to stand out, especially with this being my first video. My mission was definitely not accomplished, and I vowed to step my game up on the next video.

If You Got It,
Flaunt It

Simone was the woman who changed my life and my view of men as I knew it. I met her on the set of rapper Jason-G's video, my second shoot. I planned for this to be my make-up for the first video failure, but it ended up teaching me a whole new lesson. We were in the same scene with the rapper. She seemed to show him more attention, outshining me, and he seemed to be feeling her more.

I was envious of her receiving most of the attention and was even more furious when I overheard Jason-G say in her ear, "Come to my trailer, baby."

I watched the two secretly head toward his trailer when we were done shooting the scene. I don't know what happened, but Simone came out of the trailer with a wide smile on her face and cash in her hand. She tucked it into her pocket and winked at me as she passed by. I wanted so desperately to ask her what happened. But how stupid would I look asking her that? She went over to three of her video-girl friends by the snack table and bragged about her escapade. I walked over and pretended to get something to eat, when in reality, I was eavesdropping.

She had given Jason-G oral sex, and in return he gave her a measly three hundred dollars. I rolled my eyes. *Damn, if I was to do that I would've gotten more than three hundred dollars. That's on a crack-whore's status! Cheap ho*, I thought.

After we shot the next two scenes, Simone and I had "alone time" over in a trailer where we were getting dressed into another outfit. We had time to chat, young lady to young lady, instead of video-girl to video-girl.

"Man, I can't wait till this shoot is over," I said.

"Who you telling? I'm hungry as hell, and the fruit and raw vegetables they serving on the table ain't cutting it. I need me some damn Popeye's chicken!" Simone joked.

"I know that's right," I agreed. "I'm going to the mall to go shopping after this. I seen this cute shirt in Forever 21 that I want to buy."

"Not the shoes I want," Simone answered. She obviously didn't catch that. I was getting on the measly-ass one hundred dollars Jason-G gave her for her oral.

"Uh-huh," I said. "This shoot is kinda fun, isn't it?"

"Yes, it is, ooh yes, it is!" Simone squealed and licked her lips. She looked up as if she had seen an angel. "Jason-G is a nice guy."

"Well, I don't know him personally, and from the shoot, I still wouldn't know because he was all over you," I said, not wanting to give her too much credit for working this damn video shoot.

Simone laughed. "Check this right here, lady. I'm sure you'll continue to do more videos in the future. Who knows? You may move on to bigger and better things. Let me lay down the rules."

"Girl, what are you talking about?" I asked, yet in my mind I had taken out a pen and paper.

"Rule one: It's about the cash, not the man. Nowadays a man is only good for two things, providing sexually and providing financially. Rule two: It pays to play. If you messing around with a guy then make sure he has some money . . . and you spend it, girl! Don't give it up unless he's giving it up. You got that?"

I nodded my head. "Yeah, I hear you talking," I said nonchalantly. I tried to play it off like what she was saying was bullshit, but it was some real shit that I was digging and wanted to get in on.

"But I need you to listen, girl," Simone said, like she was my mother or something. "Rule three: If opportunity comes around, take it. Example? What I did with Jason-G! I had an opportunity to mess with it, and I did. If you were up on the game, you could have had him too. Rule four: Be flyy and shine! You gotta outshine all these other hoes, even those that ain't on the same mission. Draw the brotha's attention to you. N'a mean?"

"Yeah," I said, breathing in every word she was saying. "What else do I need to know?"

"All right, last rule," Simone began. "Rule five: Play or be played. I'm telling you, sista, don't let them use you, you use them. Get their asses before they get you. Some of these guys want one thing, and we ladies want one thing too. We have power over what they want, which is the pussy. We can use that, to get the thing we want—the cash."

I don't know what it was, but something in Simone's game had me ready to play it. I made a promise that I'd win it. I welcomed myself to the gold digger's society.

Li'l Turf

"Kirrah?" Benny said, knocking on my door.

I opened the door. "Benny? What did I tell you about showing up unannounced and uninvited?"

Benny made his way in. "Relax, babe," he said, taking his shades and raising them above his blond hairline. "I just got off the phone with Li'l Turf's agent, and he wants you to be on the set of his new video."

"Li'l Turf from New Orleans?" I asked.

"Yes. You're going to do it, right?" Benny asked as he sat on my sofa.

"You know it. Sheeeit, the Li'l Turf? I'll be in that video. When are they shooting?" I asked, looking in the mirror.

"They start shooting tonight on Manchester and Normandie at the Louisiana Fried Chicken," Benny replied.

"What song is it? Is it the 'New New Orleans' song?" I asked, hoping it was. That was my favorite song on his album. Once it started getting nationwide radio play, it became everyone's favorite.

"Yup, that's it. I love that jam!" Benny said.

I wanted to laugh at him, but could not bring myself to do it.

"The scene you'll be in is where he picks up a girl to come to the album release party. They're actually going to shoot at a club in Hollywood. You'll be one of the main girls in that scene too," Benny answered.

"Hmmm. What video did Li'l Turf see me in that made him wanna put me in his video?" I asked.

"Is that a trick question?" Benny rolled his blue eyes. "Stop playing around, Kirrah. Let's go."

"All right. When do I need to be ready?" I asked.

"They need you on the set by four-thirty. I suggest you get ready now, sweetheart," Benny said, cutting on my television. "I'll wait here while you do." He made himself comfortable on my sofa by taking off his shoes and lying down to watch what was on TV.

I went into my bathroom to take my shower and got dressed to leave.

We left twenty minutes before four o'clock and made it to the set on time. I went to wardrobe to see what I'd be wearing. Waiting, with my name on it and a fashion stylist next to it, was a sexy, short-collared jumpsuit with a gold belt. In the manager's hands were some five-inch gold stilettos.

"Kirrah?" she asked me.

"Yes," I answered.

"Hi, I'm Monique. This is the piece you'll be wearing for the first shoot, okay? We tried to make it look like you were a cashier at Louisiana Fried

Chicken. Li'l Turf is going to walk in and approach you," she said.

"All right," I answered.

"Hurry up and get dressed because they need you in makeup before five," Monique said.

We began shooting the video at six-thirty, and I played a super sexy cashier taking Li'l Turf's order. As he rapped, I danced my ass off in that cute little jumpsuit and stilettos. Li'l Turf's hands would often feel all over my body, making me forget that we were on camera and shooting his video. I knew it was going down because I could tell he wanted me. I was feeling him!

We relocated to Hollywood, and me and the other video girls changed into flashier dresses for the party scene. I was one of the three girls with Li'l Turf and his entourage in the VIP section. I was filmed walking into the club and into the VIP.

I sat down on Li'l Turf's lap and started dancing to the banging beat.

"And cut! That's a wrap!" the director yelled.

We applauded and celebrated a little more.

Li'l Turf pulled my arm, and I bent over to see what he wanted. "You gon' meet me at the hotel after this?" he asked.

"Take my number down," I said, thinking about everything Simone had told me a month ago.

I told Turf my number, and he put it in his phone. I had a wide smile on my face. *This is how it's done*, I thought.

After everyone winded down and the set was taken down, I met Turf at the Embassy Suites, the hotel near the airport, where he told me he was staying at.

I walked into the entry of the hotel and took out my cell phone to call Li'l Turf on the number he had last called me from. There was no need to go through with the call when I saw him and two of his homeboys chatting in the hotel lobby. I slowly approached him from behind.

His boy looked at me and pointed. He said to Li'l Turf, "Turf, this you?"

"Yeah," Turf said slowly after turning around and seeing me. "I'll holla at y'all later."

Li'l Turf and I went up to the elevator and to his room. Once we got in there, he lit a blunt and poured us something to drink.

Once the weed and drink set in, I found myself giving him some magnificent head while he smoked a second blunt.

"Oh sheeeeiiiit!" he moaned right before he came.

I proceeded to the bathroom to spit it out in the sink. I rinsed my mouth out and went back into the room. He signaled me to ride him. I took off my skirt and thong and slid down on his dick. I rode the country out of him and made him come into the condom twenty minutes later.

I hung out in the hotel room for the next half-hour, just entertaining Li'l Turf with my good company. We drank a little more, and I got to talking about how what happened was strictly between him and me.

"Look, I don't want you to get the wrong idea, but on some real shit, what just happened in this room stays in this room. You don't have to worry about me writing a book or ratting off at the mouth about this. Hell, I don't want anybody getting a negative opinion of me. So, hey, you don't tell, I don't tell," I said.

Li'l Turf took a wad of cash out of his pocket.

I shook my head and refused the money, knowing he would insist on giving it to me anyway. This was all part of my strategy. I had to be careful with some of these rappers, though, I was almost sure that if I refused the money from some of them, they would accept that answer and not break me off.

"Nah, I mean you were good and you got a sweet-ass pussy, but I ain't into the whole relationship with video-girls," Li'l Turf said.

Is that right? I thought to myself. *You got some nerve, Turf, because I never said that I wanted to be with your ol' country ass. I just want that money, homie.*

I watched him count off seven hundred and fifty dollars and extend it toward me. I took the money and put it the pocket of my skirt, which was on the floor.

"Just take it and buy yourself something nice," Li'l Turf said. "This don't make you no ho or nothing, so don't assume that."

Sleeping with your other rapper friends does. There ain't no shame in my game, I thought. A wide smile spread across my face and I said, "Aw, thank you."

Before gathering my things and leaving, I engaged in a common conversation with Li'l Turf, real name Eugene Goodrich. Thank the Lord for stage names! To my amusement, Li'l Turf was a Southern gentleman who was well-mannered. This was something that was not apparent within his music and lyrics. But using *ma'am* and *gorgeous* instead of *bitch* and *ho* wouldn't guarantee a *bronze* album.

Time went by so fast! What was really an hour's conversation seemed like ten minutes. I left the hotel and felt like we had made a connection . . . but it wasn't strong enough to stop my grind.

The Midwest Hustlers

The other girls and I watched them enter the room. They were all sexy in their own way. Whichever one I got close to would be the night's victim.

There was the light, bright, and just-right boy with the slick, silky ponytail and turquoise eyes from Cleveland, Ohio. They called him Superman. There was Mr. Tall, Dark, and Handsome, Grind, from Chicago. Next was Mr. Naptown, brown-skinned with thin dreads touching his shoulder and favoring Eazy-E in the face, but coming straight out of Indianapolis, Indiana. Last, but not least, there was Pretty Boy *J*, who was caramel-skinned, but had dark eyes and long braids in his hair, reppin' St. Louis. Together they were the Midwest Hustlers who were putting out club hits left and right.

We were on the set of their video "Take It to the Head." The video-girls stayed silent as we lined up like broads for sale to be chosen to be a main chick in the next couple of shots. Bianca, Yalonda,

Cherish, and I were chosen. I would be on Superman's arm.

We approached the set of the next scene. As soon as the cameras began rolling, I began rolling my hips and shaking my ass, causing Superman to be more into me than the camera. We had to shoot so many shots over again, because he couldn't lip-synch properly with me being all over him. I flirted with him throughout the day, on and off camera. It got me somewhere because he invited me to come to their room later on that night around ten.

I went home, changed into some Tru Religion jeans and a cute tank top, threw on my Louis Vuitton stilettos, and left my house. I arrived at the hotel around ten-thirty. I went up to the room he informed me they would be in. The music was so loud, I knocked repeatedly until someone answered the door.

It was a female, Bianca to be exact. Five more women were in the hotel, including Yalonda and Cherish. Everyone seemed to be having a good time. There was drink, weed, and a camera that Grind was recording the festivities with.

I spent no time waiting to get in where I fit in. I grabbed me a cup of alcohol and hit the blunt nearest to me. I found Superman on the bed talking to a half-naked female. He was taking pictures of her on his phone. I was a little disappointed because Superman had asked me to come, yet he was with another chick. But I remembered that I was only there for two things—good sex and cash. So I played the game.

I went over to him and kissed his cheek. "What's good?" I asked.

He seemed surprised, but delighted. "What's good, Kirrah?"

That's music to my ears! He's calling me by name, I thought. "Shit, just chilling. Came up here to see you. I'm a li'l tipsy, a li'l high, and I'm feeling horny," I said, thinking it was better to put the thought out there now.

Superman laughed. "Yeah, I know how you feel. Both me and Stacey," he said and pointed to the woman on the bed.

Damn, he knows her name too? Ugh! Oh well, Kirrah, play the game.

I stripped out of my jeans and my shirt. "I know you wanna take some pictures of *me* on your phone!" I sat down on the bed next to Stacey.

"Yeah, shit! Let me get some pictures of y'all two."

Stacey and I took the pictures anyway he wanted us to. Feeling it was time to make the move, I leaned in and kissed him. Because he was shitty drunk, this made the opportunity more available.

"Stacey?" I asked. "Girl, you think he ready for us?" I beckoned her over toward Superman and me.

She flung her long brown hair over her shoulders and gave him a seductive look with her hazel brown eyes. "It's only one way to find out," she said.

"Oh, well damn. That's how I get down. Let me go hit Pretty Boy *J* up for some condoms. Y'all get it wet for me. I'll be right back," Superman said, heading out of the room.

"Hurry back, daddy," I said as he left, then I looked at Stacey. "So what are you here for?"

"Relation, not relationship," she stated.

I slapped her a high-five. "I hear you talking, sista. Girl, this nigga is super drunk too. He is making it too easy."

"Don't forget that he young too! Only nineteen! Girl, I tried to make a pass at an older rapper. Girl, he got me good. He gave me the dick and then gave me a demo CD!" She laughed. "I mean, the least his rich ass could've done was given me the whole CD. What the fuck I'ma do with a demo!"

She had me cracking up with laughter. When Superman entered the room with a gold Magnum condom, we quickly straightened up and got back down to business. We made a spot in between us for him to sit down. We simultaneously stripped ourselves naked.

"Hey, baby," Stacey whispered seductively in his ear. "How much you gon' break us off if we do the shit out of you?"

I could see Superman's imprint through his shorts. I knew there was more to the meaning of his name other than that it was his favorite superhero. He was stiff as a board.

He answered. "Shit, it's nothing to my pockets. How much y'all want?"

Stacey looked at me. I answered on our behalf. "Fifteen hundred each."

She nodded her head in approval. "So what's gonna happen?" She ran her fingers along his neck as I started to slide down his shorts.

He quickly got up, went to the closet, and dug

deep into his duffle bag. His hand came out with a brick of cash. Stacey and I knew it was more than three thousand dollars. Our eyes lit up.

"You gotta do this shit right here real good," he said as his shorts dropped to the floor.

Stacey and I prepared ourselves for a night we either would or would not remember for more reasons than one. Either it would be too crazy to forget, or we'd get too drunk to remember.

After we had sexed Superman to sleep, Stacey and I counted the cash and distributed it evenly among ourselves. Each of us was going to walk away with two thousand dollars in our pockets.

The next morning, each girl in the hotel gathered herself and her things, left the hotel, and returned to her normal life as if the previous night had never happened.

As The Roman Does

Benny grabbed my arm anxiously as I came out of the dressing room, causing me to wonder what it was that had him excited. Rare.

"Kirrah, I don't know what it is, but you got it!" Benny said as he escorted me to Roman's room.

"Benny? What are you talking about?" I asked, pulling away from him.

"Of all twenty girls on the set, Roman points you out to the directors and producers. They approached me and said that Roman wants you to be on the cover of his new CD, *When In Rome!*" he exclaimed.

I squealed, "Hell, yeah!" A wide smile spread across my face. "Are you serious?"

"Dead-ass! Roman wants to meet you. Go on in!" Benny said, knocking on Roman's door.

"Who is it?" Roman asked.

"Benny and Kirrah," Benny answered, looking at me with his blue eyes sparkling with success.

Roman opened the door slowly, and I beheld the R&B phenomenon. Roman grew up in Brooklyn, New York and had the strong accent to match. His mother was Italian and his father was black, making him an exotic and classic breed. He had smooth and clear tan skin with dark, captivating eyes and black wavy hair. He was built with a solid body, and his masculine stature of six-one made girls fall in love with him even more. He was damn near perfect.

Roman hit the music world by storm with his debut album, *The Godfather*, and his number one song, "The Don of Brooklyn." He was about to be back on the scene with another hit, *When In Rome*.

Roman invited Benny and I in to talk business. He wanted me to be on the cover of the sophomore album with him. He said he liked how I carried myself on the set and that he loved my look.

After we talked business, Roman asked Benny if he and I could be alone. Benny was glad to leave us alone and left the room.

"So, Kirrah, where are you from?" he asked sitting down on the white Italian leather sofa.

"Inglewood, California," I answered proudly.

"Really? Have you ever been outside the country?" Roman asked, making room for me to sit down.

I sat down next to him and answered, "No, can't say that I have."

"You should visit Rome. My mom moved back there about three years ago. My dad is still in Brooklyn."

"I don't have the money. Where do you stay?" I asked.

"I have a penthouse in Manhattan, a mansion in

Italy, and a condo in LA," he answered, almost bragging.

I nodded my head attentively. "Where are you at the most?"

"Los Angeles because of music," Roman said. "I would love to see you outside of work sometime, Kirrah. Would you be down for that?"

I would be down for anything, literally, I thought. "We can definitely hang out sometime." As a lover of compliments, I asked Roman, "What makes me so attractive to you?"

Roman pondered before answering and then responded, "You are a special kind of beauty—It's not something you come across all the time—because you're unique. You came on the set and it felt good. It felt good to be around you, and it feels good now. The only reason why people see you all the time is because you're in almost every artist's video. You're a hit, really. You have the milk-chocolate skin, the pretty black hair, those almond-shaped eyes, and your body is flawless."

I smiled when I really wanted to stand up and dance in the mirror. After a person hears that they look good so many times, it has to go to the head, because it has nowhere else to go. "Aw, thank you. I wasn't one of the girls who was told that in high school," I lied.

"The guys at your school must've been blind or gay," he said. "So, what are you doing tomorrow? I have the day to myself, but I would love to share it with you."

"Nothing," I answered.

Roman and I exchanged numbers, something I was glad about, because I had to get close to him.

Something about him intrigued me. Maybe it was his features or his practical nature.

The next morning, Roman called me bright and early and made sure I was ready for our date. He saw me in my mid-thigh Giorgio Armani dress. I wore my Anne Klein sandals, to add a springy touch. I hopped into his black Rolls Royce, and he gave me a kiss on the cheek.

"You look gorgeous, Kirrah!" Roman said.

I giggled. "Aw, thank you, Roman! You look good in your outfit. And you smell good too!"

"That would be Antonio Banderas for Men, baby girl," he replied, pulling away from my Inglewood apartment. "Have you been to San Diego?"

"Um, once. When I went to the beach."

"Well, that's where we are headed. The beach! This ought to be a fun date. I'm going to show you my favorite view of the ocean. You'll see why it's my favorite."

"Sounds fun," I fibbed. "I'm excited!"

"Yeah, I think this is step one of a really good relationship. I'm pretty sure we'll be working very close in the future, and I really like you," Roman said. "Of course, I got to get to know you a bit more! I hope you are sincere!"

If you only knew, I thought grinning.

Whip It!

"Oh, Roman! I like it. No, I love it!" I said, beholding the silver two-seater Porsche parked in front of my apartment. A red bow was on the hood, with a tag reading To KIRRAH attached to it.

"I knew you would, baby," Roman said, lifting me off the ground in a hug. "Go smell the inside."

I loved the smell of a new car. I raced to the driver's seat, hopped in, inhaled deeply, and exhaled in appreciation. I was definitely playing the game with a good hand.

I had been nine months into a relationship with Roman, and I had a new ride. I had been loyal, so far, to Roman in what he called "a beautiful union." But I called it a temporary stop in my game. Roman was my biggest catch yet. Of course I had to take my time with him. I was the perfect celebrity girlfriend, basking in the fame, dodging paparazzi, and respecting Roman's popularity. My shit had to be on point. Simone would be so damn proud of me, and jealous too!

I hopped out of the car and ran back into Roman's arms and followed that with a hug and a sensual kiss. "Ooh, you're gonna get some tonight, baby," I promised.

"Aw, baby girl, I wish I could get some, but I have to be in New York for fashion week. Think you can save it?" he asked.

"Well," I began, "I guess so."

"I want you to floss in your new ride today," Roman said. He took out his wallet and handed me a couple of hundreds. "Spend freely. I transferred some money to your account yesterday."

"Really? Thank you. How much?" I asked with bright eyes.

"Five thousand," he said.

I frowned. "Honey, that won't even get me the bag I want in Beverly Hills."

He put a kiss on my forehead. "I'm just playing, Kirrah. It's more than enough to last you a couple of days."

"What if I run out?" I asked.

"Call me," Roman responded. He walked me back inside the apartment.

"At least let me get some before you go," I begged him. "Please?" I pulled him toward the bedroom.

"Okay, *mamacita*. All right."

Roman and I made love at that instant. At the moment, I actually felt like his true woman. But, in reality, I was just his undoing. I almost felt sorry that I was playing him so hard. But a gold digger's gotta do what an ordinary girl can't do.

After Roman left my apartment, I got dressed

into something flyy. I had to be seen in my new Porsche. I called my cousin VaRhonda and told her I was on my way.

"Who is dropping you off?"

"Girl, I got a new ride," I said. "A Porsche!"

"Get your ass over here. I gotta see this to believe it!" VaRhonda exclaimed.

I got over to her apartment on West Queen Street as soon as I could. She met me outside and was shocked when she saw me step out of the Porsche.

"Believe it, girl!" I said, fanning myself. "Ain't it flyy?"

"Roman's money, huh?" VaRhonda joked as she ran her hands along the doors of my new car.

"But my tricks," I bragged. "I'm taking all the credit. I basically worked for this."

"Girl, I shoulda been a video-ho." VaRhonda laughed. "I just cashed my check, so you know what I'm ready to do."

"And Roman just put some money in my account. So let's go," I said. "Where you wanna go?" I asked, getting into the driver's seat.

"Take me right up the street to the Inglewood Swap Meet, Kirrah. I gotta get my kids some shoes," VaRhonda said.

"Inglewood Swap Meet? Girl, I got Hollywood money," I whined.

"Well, I got swap-meet dough. Bitch, don't act like you too good for the hood. It ain't you who's rich, it's Roman," VaRhonda said, giving me a reality check.

The reality was, I was messing with a rich man,

and as long as he was mine, the money was mine. "Well, I'm going to floss my shit," I said, starting up my car, "not at the Inglewood Swap Meet."

"Girl, fuck that. I need to get my kids some shoes 'cuz they deadbeat daddy can't afford shit," VaRhonda said.

"'Cuz they deadbeat daddy is in and out of jail for hitting on they mama," I corrected.

VaRhonda sucked her teeth and answered, "Girl, please. I kicked his ass out for good. Believe that!"

I laughed at her. "VaRhonda, he'll be right back up in there in a couple of days, maximum. The whole family knows it. You addicted to that abuse."

"Well, me being addicted to an abusive man is just like you being addicted to sex."

"Hold up, cousin. Get it right. It isn't sex that I'm addicted to, it's the money. All right?"

She shook her head. "Anyways," she stated, "don't try to call me out."

I left it at that. We arrived at the Inglewood Swap Meet, and I drove past the crowded entry, passing the parking lot entrance so I could be seen.

"Damn, you ballin'!" one of the guys shouted at me.

I responded to him with a smile. *You're not*, I thought, my million-dollar smile on.

"You a little conceited wench." VaRhonda giggled. "You ain't Hollywood status. You just upper Inglewood."

I laughed and said, "I'm all that and more, Va-Rhonda. Don't hate."

Played for a Fool

"I gotta go, Camden," I moaned as he pleasured me. "I gotta go home. Ooh, this feels so good, Camden!"

Camden muffled, "Nah, you gotta let me taste this some more, baby. Just a little more."

I quivered uncontrollably as I came closer and closer to exploding. "Camden, no baby! Noooooooooooo!" I screeched as I reached my peak.

He snickered as he cleaned me up with his tongue. "That's how we do it in New Jersey," he bragged.

"Well, maybe I need to move to the East Coast," I said.

Camden sighed and said, "Maybe you should. Are you joining me in the shower?"

"Nah, I'm gonna lay here and rest a little bit."

Camden shrugged his shoulders and walked over toward the table in the hotel room. He took his wallet out of his pocket, removed his chain, and placed both items on the table. "I won't be long. You sure you don't wanna join me?" he asked one more time.

"I'm sure, Camden," I replied sweetly.

Camden got naked and went into the bathroom, closing the door behind him.

I got up, put my clothes on, and walked over to the table. I dug through his wallet and took three hundred dollars.

Camden, NJ's finest rapper, is a little short on the dough, I thought as I left the hotel room. In the car on my ride home, I hoped I would have enough time to clean myself up and get to Roman's condo before he got home.

I arrived at my house and got myself clean by showering the scent and touch of another artist off of my body. I put some Victoria's Secret lotion on, changed into something sexy, and left my apartment. I drove to Roman's condo in The Hills, parking two houses down so he would not see my car. I wanted him to be surprised.

I walked to the front door and located the spare key under a flowerpot. I opened the door and made myself at home.

To welcome Roman home, I lit vanilla-scented candles all over the house. With daylight savings time in effect, it would be dark as night by six PM. Roman should be walking in by six-thirty PM. I cooked up a nice bowl of angel hair pasta. Roman would adore me when he found me here in his home, being the perfect girlfriend.

At six thirty-eight, I heard his car pull into the garage. I hid in the bedroom and waited for him to enter.

I heard Roman come into his condo with the beautiful actress, London Falls, by his side.

"Oh, Roman!" she said, flinging her arms around him. "You had this planned just for me!" She inhaled the scent that the warm vanilla candles offered.

"Hey, London, are you hungry? Let's go get something to eat."

"Absolutely," London said. She pranced into the kitchen. "The chef did a wonderful job preparing this angel hair pasta. Yummy."

Roman ran into the kitchen. "Chef? Oh yeah, he did, huh?"

I overheard the two voices proceeding into the bedroom. When I stepped out of the bathroom, I caught them just in time. London was pulling Roman toward the bed, and in return he was pulling her toward the door.

"Honey," London said, "who is this?"

"Roman?" I asked. "Who is that?"

Roman put his hands on his waist and took a drastic sigh. I approached the situation carefully, not sure of the outcome.

"You gon' tell her who I am? Or do I have to introduce myself?" I asked.

When Roman didn't answer, I decided that it was my turn to speak again.

"All right then! I'm Kirrah. I'm Roman's girlfriend, ten months strong. Might I ask, who the hell are you?"

She looked at Roman for guidance. Should she answer? She looked at me and said, "Actress London Falls. "Roman, you told me you and Kirrah were over."

I knew the bitch was an actress. I just wanted to come at her in a way that would show she wasn't running anything.

"Don't be a smart ass," I stated. "Roman, I think you have some explaining to do to this 'supporting' actress." I looked him up and down. "Don't try to play me for no damn fool. Roman, handle that and get at me when you done fooling around with her."

I walked out of the room and into the kitchen to throw the pasta in the trashcan. Next, I blew out every single candle I had lit. *So that's how it feels to be cheated on*, I thought. *This is fucked up!*

Romancing Roman

The next day, I received several phone calls from Roman. Each time, I sent him straight to the answering machine. He left me messages begging me to pick up the phone and tell him I forgive him. He swore to me that he made London leave right after he told her about me, soon after I left his house. He wanted another chance and was ready to do anything I commanded.

This was my victory. I could now have Roman eating out of the palm of my hand. Now that Roman had done me wrong, I could use it as an excuse to say he should give me anything I wanted.

I returned his phone calls the day after. "Roman," I said when he picked up the phone on the first ring.

"Oh, baby," he said. "I'm sorry, Kirrah. London and I didn't do anything. She means nothing to me. I love you, Kirrah."

Love me? I thought, *Ooh, this is easier than I thought. Keep going.*

As if reading my mind, Roman continued, "You

are perfect. You are the most perfect girl in the world. I want to be with you. Really, I do. Kirrah, baby, please. I hope you forgive me. I really want to work this out."

I let him speak his mind till he almost wailed. I felt I had won this guy, his money, and more.

"Speak to me, Kirrah," he requested.

With an honest tongue, I said, "I want to go shopping."

"Okay, baby! I'm on the way over there! Anything you want is yours, Kirrah!"

Roman came to my house and picked me up in his new ride, a Bentley coupe.

I got into the passenger seat. When he leaned over to kiss me, I moved away. I didn't want him to think that I had let him off the hook that easily. There was more to it.

Roman and I went to the Ontario Mills Mall, in Ontario. The ride was devoid of chatter. Roman didn't know what to say, and I didn't speak because there wasn't much to say at that point. First we'd go to the mall, do a little shopping, go out to dinner and then we'd talk.

At the mall, I made Roman splurge. I made him buy me clothes, shoes, and accessories.

Roman questioned if I'd had enough yet. I felt as if he was trying to challenge me by saying that he could buy me the whole world and more. I accepted this challenge and asked for three more pairs of shoes—two stilettos and a pair of Nikes.

"Where do you want to eat?" Roman put the shopping bags into the trunk of his car.

"Olive Garden," I answered.

"Italian food, huh?"

"Yup," I said. "Is that a problem?"

Roman shook his head. "Baby, you're looking at an Italian man. I can cook you some Italian food if you asked me to."

"But I didn't," I snapped. I rolled my eyes, folded my arms, and sat back in the leather car seat.

Roman sucked his teeth. He got angry and said, "Kirrah, look, I don't need your attitude right now. I'm trying to make up for what I did wrong. The way you're acting is not helping that."

"Don't give me that bullshit. We wouldn't even be in this situation if your ass didn't bring that D-list actress to your house. Don't try to twist this shit!"

"Kirrah, I have apologized!" Roman yelled. "And what the hell were you doing at my house anyway?"

"I wanted to surprise you! Is it my fault I missed your cheating ass?" I screamed.

"You know what?" Roman asked. "Fuck this shit! I don't need this! We're going home. This is too much. Any other girl would've let this go, this time. I'm busting my ass trying to get shit right with you. You don't wanna be with me? Then it's done! It's over!"

Aw shit! I thought as I realized Roman leaving me meant the end of my financial well. Now what the hell was I supposed to do? Trying to stay mad at Roman didn't work out the way it was supposed to.

So what did I do? I put on the don't-leave-me act. I began crying, my best performance yet. "Roman! You're going to leave me? And it was you who did me wrong? How you gon' do that to me? Roman, I loved you. But you can't play me. What was I supposed to think was going on between you and London? Roman, I can't believe you. I thought you loved me! How can you do this to me?"

Roman panicked. He didn't even start the car up. He just put his arms around me and apologized for yelling at me and saying that the relationship was over.

"I'm not just any other girl! I'm Kirrah, baby! I wasn't gonna let you get away with it, because I love you. I wanted you to see I was hurt!" I boo-hooed.

"Yes, baby, I know. I'm sorry. I see that you're hurting. I won't ever do anything stupid like that again! I apologize, Kirrah," Roman said. "Do you forgive me, baby girl?"

I nodded my head. "Yes," I said in a low tone. "Can we go eat now, Roman?"

Roman chuckled and answered, "Yes, Kirrah, we can go eat."

I felt it necessary to hold onto Roman because he was so into me. During the rest of our relationship, I played him silly.

I kept doing my music videos and started hooking up with other artists again. I had Dee Boy from Houston, Texas—boy broke me off with some country dick and some city cash. I had *Guapo* from Cuba. He was my Cuban lover and blessed me with *mucho dinero*! Many more artists became names on my list, and money in my pocket. And to think I did all of it while still romancing Roman, who continued to spoil me rotten, taking care of any financial situations I made up and sexing me crazy.

Little did I know, my promiscuous ways and gold digging nature would put me in some life-altering situations and make me reevaluate every step I took.

Tracing Back

It was a windy afternoon on a Wednesday. Benny and I were returning from Malibu Beach for a magazine shoot. I would've gone by myself, but Benny insisted on coming to see the other models. After the shoot, we decided to grab lunch at a restaurant nearby.

Now we were on the 405 freeway, heading back to my home. Benny had his pedal to the metal as he did eighty-five miles an hour. His favorite Jay-Z song, "Show Me What You Got," blasted from the car stereo. He said the song reminded him of drag racing.

"Roman bought me a Juicy Couture necklace. It's too cute, Benny," I said, making conversation.

"You sure do have him whipped, don't you?" Benny asked.

"Hey, what can I say?" I bragged. "I got the magic touch. Gave him some once and he's been hooked ever since."

"You have him thinking that you're a faithful and

sincere woman. You devil!" Benny laughed. "Meanwhile, you're hooking up with other artists and taking their money as a thank-you note!"

"Yeah, I know," I said. "It's a fucked-up process, but somebody's gotta be the villain. Good girls always finish last."

Benny shook his head. "Kirrah, sweetheart," he began, "now I understand you're on your . . . what do you call it? *Grind.* I hope you're keeping up with your men more than you're keeping up with the money."

"What are you talking about?" I asked. I wanted him to spare me the drama and be blunt.

"Are you making these clowns wear a condom?" Benny asked. It was a random question, but I knew he was truly concerned.

"Um, well, some of them," I answered truthfully.

"Who?" Benny asked.

"I don't remember! Most of them don't, though, not on purpose. But don't worry. They pull out before cumming, and I'm taking birth control."

Benny gasped like he was scared of me. "Kirrah! I'm not talking about you getting pregnant! I'm talking about you getting an STD!"

"Kirrah getting an STD? Now what made you think of that?" I asked, taking into consideration what he was saying, but not wanting to let it get to my head.

"As sexually active as you are, it's hard *not* to think like that," Benny answered. "I care about you because you're damn near my best friend. I can talk to you about these kind of things, right?"

"Yeah, as long as you don't sound like my dad," I

answered. "You make it seem like I don't take care of myself. I'm not a little girl, Benny. I'm a woman. I do what I have to fucking do."

"Well, when was the last time you've been to the doctor?"

"Like, four months ago, damn it!" I exclaimed.

"And how many guys have you slept with since then?"

"Five hundred," I said sarcastically.

"Be serious, Kirrah," Benny said. "You're in denial."

"Oh, shut up. You know I was joking! It's been like . . . I don't know, maybe ten or something like that," I said nonchalantly.

"Something like that?" Benny repeated.

"Between ten and fifteen," I corrected. "I have a list at home."

"Kirrah, I don't mean to come down on you or butt all in your business. I just want to make sure you are taking care of your personal business while doing what you're doing," Benny said in a calm voice that soothed the anger brewing in me.

Part of me was upset with him for even coming at me the way he was. But I realized he was only doing this because he cared. Now was the time I had to put my arrogance aside and humble myself.

I put my hand over my mouth. I was slipping! I let the money get in the way of my health. I was having protected sex with *some* of these guys, but I was also having unprotected sex with *most* of them. Both me and the men were negligent. They were caught up in the pussy, and I was caught up in the paper. I hadn't been showing any signs. I didn't get fatigued or sick, nor were there any physical symptoms.

Benny and I agreed I should see my gynecologist within the next couple of days. But I set up an appointment with my gynecologist three weeks later. Although I should have done it much earlier, I needed some time to gather myself. The fact that I was going to the gynecologist and was nervous about it was hard to swallow. I was literally scared about this, and scared was an emotion I had not felt in a long time.

My gynecologist went through her procedures and performed a full examination. I was sent to the restroom to give her a urine sample. I returned with my sample and handed it to her. I waited for her to come back into the room. She reentered and told me to come back in two days.

When two days passed, I drove back to the office for my results. I went into the room and waited for my gynecologist to come in with the results. I was in a hurry because Roman and I were going to the movies later on that afternoon. I wanted to go home, freshen up, and be at his condo an hour before show time.

My gynecologist entered the room with a large brown folder, sat down in a chair across from me, and began asking her usual questions.

"When was the last time you were sexually active?" she asked.

"A week ago."

"Did you use protection?"

"No."

"Are you on some kind of birth control?"

"The pill, yes."

"Have you had more than one partner within the last eight months?"

Her question threw me for a loop. "Huh?"

She repeated her question.

I answered hesitantly, "Um . . . yes."

"Do you still keep in contact with them to this day?" she asked, writing something down on her paper.

"Yes," I lied. I didn't want to say no, because I didn't have time for any other questions.

"I would like for you to try to contact your previous partners that you have had sex with within the last eight months," she commanded.

I was surprised. "Why?" I asked, getting an attitude.

"Kirrah, sweetheart, you do have an STD," she answered.

The words echoed through my head as I replayed what she said over and over. I went back a couple of seconds ago to make sure I had heard her correctly. I wanted to puke. I felt violated, disgusted, and ashamed. Everything sexual that I had done in the past now seemed horrific in every kind of way.

"WHAT?" I screamed. I was in a rampage. I stormed around the room angrily. I asked, "Which one? Which one, damn it!?"

My gynecologist tried to soothe me. She held me like a mother holding a child to stop her from wailing. "Relax, Kirrah. Okay?"

"What do I have? Is it curable? Am I going to die?" The questions were flying out way too fast. I began to cry uncontrollably.

She answered, "Don't worry. This is what I am here for. You have contracted chlamydia. Now this is serious because, if not taken care of immediately, it can damage the reproductive system, and women infected are five times more likely to become infected with HIV. But it is curable, alright? I'm going to prescribe you a treatment called doxycycline. You take it for a week straight, Kirrah."

Chlamydia, I thought as I left the clinic. *Ugh! This is unreal! Who gave this to me?*

The question I needed to be asking was, Who did I give it to?

When I got home, I called Benny and told him the grave news. He immediately came to my house and consoled me in my desperate time of need. I bawled in his arms.

"Oh, Kirrah. What in the world happened? You should've been more careful, that's all," he said benignantly.

"Benny, I have chlamydia! How could I have been so damn stupid? Damn it, I didn't even show any signs!" I yelled, screaming to the city of Inglewood.

"Yeah, most women don't," Benny responded.

"I guess my luck ran out," I sobbed. I grabbed a tissue from the tissue box and wiped my nose. This was the third tissue box I had used up. My nose was redder than Rudolph's, and my cheeks were puffier than a baby's. I looked appalling.

"Well, is there any way for you to trace it back to your previous partners?" Benny took the snotty tissue from me and tossed it into the trashcan.

I gave him a stupid look. "NO! Then I'd really

look like a ho! You know how many guys I've had sex with?" I thought of the guys' names in my head. "Ain't no telling who the fuck I got it from, Benny!"

Mike, Li'l Turf, Superman, Camden, Guapo, Pappy, Harlem Child, T-Lo, Rocky, Dee Boy, Dayton, D-Rail, Dubbs, Cash, Davion and Roman.

There was no way I was going to contact their agents and try to get in contact with them over an STD. My name would be in the news, they would be spreading this among other hip-hop artists, and my grind would be ruined.

In a Matter of Time

The next day, I made it my personal chore to break things off with Roman until I straightened myself out. I would even make the ultimate sacrifice of putting music video gigs on pause. I would have to live off of the money in my bank account until I got back into work again. Benny vowed to help me in any way.

I called Roman and told him that we would have to stop talking. Of course, he demanded to know why. I simply told him it was because of some personal issues I had been going through. I would get back to him when I was revitalized (and clear of the STD) for sure.

About two days later I saw a picture in the tabloids with him and London Falls at a restaurant in New York City. The article made mention of their engagement.

It was all good. I was pissed off because Roman had fooled me yet again, as I had fooled him this whole time. Therefore, I deserved it. I was even more pissed off that my hustle had to come to an unwanted stop. I had messed myself up big time and was humiliated at the consequences.

But, I'd be back to my old ways, this time being more careful and carrying my own stack of rubbers. I'd be back to gold digging . . . all in a matter of time.

Over the next seven days, Benny had me on what he called "labor rest." I was not booked for any videos or photo shoots and found myself deprived of work. Truth of the matter was, I still wanted to shoot music videos and photos for magazines. But I appreciated the fact that Benny had my best interest at heart, even if it meant denying me a gig. Benny proved himself a loyal friend throughout my hard time. With everything going on, he stayed the same old Benny. Benny was faithfully taking care of me with groceries, meals, and other things.

I only had chlamydia, not cancer. It bugged me out that he was showing so much generosity, almost too much generosity. It became aggravating to the point I just started cursing him out every time he tried to help me. I thought that would've stopped him from helping out so much. Instead, it only encouraged him to give me books on inner peace and tranquility.

"Girl, I can't take it!" I said to VaRhonda after she called me on a late Wednesday night. "Benny just became a maid and I can't stand it. You ever heard of help just being too much? The man acts like I can't do a gotdamn thing on my own!"

"He's just tryin'a be there for you. You know Benny is secretly in love with you," VaRhonda teased.

"Girl, shut that shit up right now! Benny ain't in love with me at all. He is my agent and that's that!" I protested. "I'm surprised the muthafucka ain't here right now holding the phone for me."

"Oh, don't speak too soon. He could be right around the way," VaRhonda said.

"Is that supposed to be another joke? 'Cuz if it is, it ain't funny," I said.

"Eww, you are grouchy, girl," VaRhonda replied. "Lighten up. What ever happened to 'it's just chlamydia'?"

"Just chlamydia" became my philosophy because I refused to let it end my hustle and damage my pride. I was still flyy on the outside, just flaming on the inside. I just had to cure myself of chlamydia and return to the scene.

"VaRhonda, I'm gonna call you back," I said. I got off the phone with her and thought about my career and opportunities.

I had only been in the house for two days, and it felt like two weeks. Benny had me on this bullshit "labor rest" and was being the worst agent ever. I gave him a call.

"Benny? Why the hell haven't you been booking me for videos or photo shoots?" I yelled into the phone.

"Kirrah, I want you to get completely rid of it before you go back into that," Benny said.

"Oh my goodness, Benny! I have been using my treatment! I want to get back to my job!" I said, getting upset with him. "I have till the end of the week. But that doesn't mean I can't model and shit!"

Benny sighed into the phone. "Kirrah, I think you need to handle this situation right now."

"You know what, Benny? You're really getting on my Inglewood nerves right now! I'm above this chlamydia shit! Okay? Why you ain't putting me in no videos? You think I'm gon' sleep around some more?" I yelled.

"I don't know. I mean, after all, sleeping around is what got you into this mess," Benny replied.

"Oh, fuck you, Benny! You so full of shit that it stinks! How am I supposed to make my damn money?"

"Who has been taking care of you, Kirrah? Anything you need, I got you!" Benny said. And he was right. "Kirrah, you are so young and you want the world to revolve around you, but it can't. Now your fast ways got you in some shit that you're slow to get out of. You need to take care of yourself."

"You need to be my agent and not my father!" I snapped.

"I'm trying to be a friend!"

"Well, don't!" I screamed.

There was an eerie silence; the kind of silence where someone just said something that they should not have and it shocks both people.

Benny cleared his throat and said, "Kirrah, if you go back to doing the same thing you were doing, you can get worse. What if you get another STD? Like AIDS? People die from that shit you know! Hello, Eazy-E?"

I sucked my teeth. "Eazy-E was a sucker who wasn't strapping up!"

"So then what does that make you?"

"It makes me lucky that I ain't get that serious of an STD!"

"You can be so stupid sometimes, little girl!" Benny mumbled.

"Little girl?! Benny, I am twenty-one years old! I am grown! Don't call me a little girl! Why you gotta go there? Is it 'cuz I'm black? Huh, Benny? Your white ass thinks you tha massuh and I'm a slave? All you are is an agent!" I ranted.

Benny responded, "Don't play the race card, Kirrah. That's bullshit and you know it! Now, you're just crazy! I respect you as Kirrah, a person, a lady. I wouldn't care if you were black, pink, or purple!"

"Then get my black, pink, or purple ass in a video," I demanded.

"Whoa, ho, ho," Benny said sarcastically. "Who's the massuh now?"

"Don't fuck with me, Benny," I warned. "I will fire your ass."

"You'll fire me? For what? Caring about you when those rappers could give a damn if you're dead or alive?"

"Don't test me."

"I'm not testing you. I am telling you," Benny responded.

"Telling me what?"

"I fucking quit!" Benny hung up, making me more upset than I had ever been.

I realized once again that I would have to return to my hustle (this time on my very own) and be that flyy bitch . . . only in a matter of time.

Word Is . . .

Shit was so fucked-up once Benny was gone. Career-wise, I felt alone and miserable. On top of that, it was only day five of the seven-day process. Though I only had two more days, time seemed to be going by so slowly.

During times like these, I needed a night out with VaRhonda. I called her up and asked her if she wanted to hit the club. Snatching up any opportunity to leave her kids and baby daddy behind, VaRhonda gladly accepted. I told her I was about to get ready and in about an hour I would be at her door.

A little over an hour, she opened the door and let me in. She had put the kids in bed and her baby daddy was laid out on the couch watching videos on MTV2. VaRhonda had on an Inglewood Swap Meet original club outfit. She had on the "somebody's brand" denim boots with a staggering six-inch heel, a lime green halter top that bore a glittery butterfly, and a denim miniskirt that had some of the glitter the butterfly shed on it.

I wanted to laugh because in comparison to the House of Dereon short dress I was sporting, she looked downright dingy. But we were only going to The Galaxy Club on LaBrea and Manchester.

"How do I look?" VaRhonda asked as she spun around in a circle, thinking she was the shit.

"Like a fifteen-year-old," I replied truthfully. "You need to get up on some new shit!"

"Fuck you, ho. My boo thinks I look good, huh, baby?" She turned around and looked at him.

He replied, "Don't be dancing on no mutha-fuckas!"

VaRhonda rolled her eyes and asked, "Kirrah, you ready to go?"

I nodded my head. VaRhonda and I left the apartment and went down to the lot. We got into my car and headed toward the club.

We were there in what seemed like no time. We walked toward the back of the line. I eyed the dusty females and nodded my head in approval at the ones who were as flyy as me tonight.

"Yo, VaRhonda, wait right here while I try to get us in for free," I said as I switched down the side of the line toward the bouncer.

"How you doing, big daddy?" I said as I made eye contact with the three-hundred-pound–plus club bouncer patrolling the door.

"Fine, and yourself?"

"I'm good, but I would be better if I can get on up in there," I said with a laugh.

He tossed me a fake smile and said, "Sorry, sweetheart. Not tonight."

I gave him a disgusted look. I could not believe

he straight clowned me like that. I was the flyyest chick in Inglewood and I wasn't even getting in the club for half price. The people in line watched me take the walk of shame back to the line.

"What happened?" VaRhonda asked.

"Girl, that fat-ass bouncer wouldn't even let me get up in there. You see how good I look? What man wouldn't want me up in his club?" I ran my hands along my curves. "He must be a homo!"

"Is he light-skinned? Real big? With green eyes and a flat top?" VaRhonda stepped out of the line.

"Yeah, he is," I replied. "But I know you ain't gon' try to press your luck with ol' boy?"

"Kirrah, that's my homie Tiny Tommy. We went to Morningside together. Hold up while I get us up in here," VaRhonda said, walking to the front of the line.

I know VaRhonda ain't gon' get past Tiny Tommy. If I ain't make it, she definitely ain't gon' make it! And why the hell they call the guy Tiny Tommy when he big as hell? That must be the irony cuz ain't no way he tiny anywhere except down there, I thought, while VaRhonda handled her business. *Here come VaRhonda now, and she don't look like she was successful.*

"What happened? He ain't let you in, right?" I predicted it coming.

"Oh, nah, he let me in and gave me the VIP bracelets. Let's go, girl," VaRhonda said, taking my wrist and putting the bracelet on. She grabbed my hand and led me toward the entry. "See, it was that easy. Tiny Tommy just saw my face, gave me a hug, and told me to come on in. When I told him I had a friend here, he gave me the bracelets and told me to go get you."

"Uh huh," I said with a tad bit of jealousy. "That's all good."

We whizzed past Tiny Tommy's fat ass and entered the club.

The club was popping, as a club should be. I hoped the front door incident wasn't an indication of what the whole night would be like for me. I be damned if VaRhonda was more popular than me tonight.

We went to the bar to get a little alcohol in our system. I wouldn't be drinking unless someone was paying for it. I hadn't been to the club in the last five months, so of course I wanted to see if I still had it. I watched VaRhonda order a drink.

She looked at me. "Am I the only one drinking tonight, designated driver?" she asked as she sipped on her Green Hulk.

I gave her the "*girl, please!*" look. "Yeah, right! I'm gonna drink tonight, but I'm gonna have a guy pay for it. I refuse to spend any of my money," I answered as I looked around the club for any men with potential.

"All righty then," VaRhonda said. "Don't wait all night. I'm going to dance after this drink." She downed the rest of her alcohol and set it on the glass bar table. "Holla back, bitch." She switched onto the dance floor, pulling a guy she knew from high school along with her.

I seriously needed to get my own entourage of flyy bitches. I knew she was my cousin and all, but VaRhonda was not flyy in any way, form, or fashion. She had some terrible badass kids and an abusive baby daddy . . . not that he was her fault, but she was still with the dumb ass.

I sat at the bar looking pretty, but feeling empty. Still, no guy had come up to approach me. I knew I looked good, so what the hell was wrong with these losers? Maybe I should have taken my ass to the gay bar and tried my luck there.

If I wasn't mistaken, I kept getting weird stares from a table crowded with four knockoff bitches. I hoped they wouldn't be the first people to talk to me. I ignored the stares, but as I glanced at them a moment later, they were still eyeing me. I finally gave up the silent treatment and grabbed a waiter.

"Excuse me, can you go over to that table and ask them broads why the hell are they staring at me like I'm some kind of art?" I snapped.

The waiter fearfully nodded his head and went to the table to ask them my question. He looked back at me, and looked back at them.

I cocked my head in disbelief. *Don't tell me he's staring too? Is there something on the back of my dress?* I sneakily felt the back of my dress to see if there was any kind of food, drink or blood even.

The waiter returned and said, "They said there was no problem. They just remembered you from some music videos and said they heard something about you."

"Well, what did they hear?" I asked angrily.

"You ought to take that up with them," the waiter said nervously.

"Thanks for no help," I said, moving the waiter out of my way and walking over to the table. I think I was walking so fast, my heels couldn't keep up. I placed my hands on the table and leaned on it for support. "So, what's the word?"

"No, this bitch didn't," the dark-skinned, Barbie-looking girl said to the friend on her left. She turned her head around as if she could not believe I had the audacity to approach them.

"Oh, yeah, I did," I snapped. "'Cuz if you got something to say, then I'm right here. What the fuck?" I put my hands on my hips.

The young lady with red hair took a sip of her drink. "C'mon now, Kirrah. Don't be all high school on us. Just go on back to the bar with your lonely ass and wait for a guy to approach you."

"How the fuck do you know my name?" I asked.

"We seen you in videos and magazines, not that that makes you a celebrity or nothing, but you are just as scandalous," Black Barbie said.

"Bitch, stop being sarcastic and say whatever you got to say. You heard something?" I asked, ready to jump over the table and slap her face backwards.

"Nothing really," the mixed chick said. "Just that you be burning niggas."

"I be burning niggas?"

"Yeah, with that STD running wild down there. Girl, it ain't no secret. Everybody in 'the Wood' knows that's why you been low-key these past couple of days. You were supposed to be at Dayton's album release party. But you couldn't come out the house, huh? It's because you got to get rid of that problem, huh?" Red Hair asked. "Word is, you gave it to Dayton."

I shook my head angrily and thought about my rendezvous with Dayton after shooting his video. Some mixed chick who went by the name of Mickey was trying to get his attention as she danced like a stripper playfully. During this time I seized the opportunity to talk to him and we hit it off from there. That night in a hotel room we had sex, and in the morning we went our separate ways. Truth of the matter was, I didn't know who I got it from, and I didn't know who I'd given it to.

I wanted to cry, but pride would not let me do it, at least not in front of these hoes. I gave all of them a threatening look and recognized the fourth girl from previous music videos.

It was Simone. My evil glare turned into rage. She was the reason why I got into all of this gold digging bullshit. I could've cursed her out for introducing me to it. To me, it was comparative to a drug dealer introducing a teenager to crack and ruining the rest of their life.

"Damn, Kirrah," Simone said. "I meant to tell you to always protect yourself." She shook her head in disappointment.

"Don't give me that bullshit," I yelled. "If it weren't for you, I would never be in this situation. You put me on the game."

"And you decided to play it. I ain't put you on nothing. I told you the rules and you rolled the dice. Don't blame me for your mistakes. You know what? If I would've stayed in contact with your ass, then I would've told you the rule about always using a condom!" Simone replied.

I sucked my teeth. "Fuck you, Simone. Fuck all y'all. Fuck what you heard! And where did you hear that bullshit lie anyway? That ain't why I been low-key," I lied.

"Well, why?" the redhead asked, trying to catch me in a lie.

"My mother was sick with cancer," I fibbed. I knew it was dirty to lie on my mom like that, but I had a reputation to maintain.

They shook their heads disappointingly.

The mixed chick answered for them all. "Miss Kirrah, that is very low. How you gon' lie on your mom like that? Girl, you are so desperate. Everybody that reads *Urban Life* magazine knows you got chlamydia."

"What do you mean, everybody that reads *Urban Life*?" I asked, as I took my hands off my hip and let them fall to my side.

Black Barbie turned to Simone and shook her head. "She really has no fucking idea about what's going on," she said as she took her drink in her hand. She placed the rim of her glass up to her lips.

Simone got up from the table, grabbed my arm gently and walked me toward the restrooms. "Look, I thought you would understand all the rules without me having to tell them to you. Every young woman, especially one as beautiful as you, should know that you need to have protected sex. Suppose you had gotten HIV or AIDS? Damn, Kirrah, you really need to be a little smarter about shit like this in the future," she said.

"Will everyone stop acting like they are my fucking parents? It's just chlamydia," I replied, shrugging my shoulders.

I wondered if it would be safe to cry in front of

her. I had been hearing the same shit from everybody that it hurt so badly. First Benny, VaRhonda, my mother, my aunt, and now Simone.

"Just chlamydia? Girl, where did you get that attitude? It don't matter what it is, you got an STD and that ain't good. It doesn't make you sexy, and it doesn't make you happy. It makes you dumb and makes you feel low, especially now that your cousin done put that shit in the open."

"What the hell?" I asked. "VaRhonda?"

"Yes," Simone replied. "VaRhonda, your cousin, contacted *Urban Life* magazine and told them she had a story about you, and they wanted to hear it. For years now many people wanted to bring you down. I know that from experience. Folks tried to bring me down, 'cuz I was going somewhere and making money. Now I might've been doing it the wrong way. But whatever way the ends meet, right? Right. Now that this little secret escaped, girl, they done brought you all the way down."

"So, let me get this straight VaRhonda went to *Urban Life* and told them about me getting chlamydia?"

"Yes, and they even approached Benny, your ex-agent, about it to see if it was true, but he declined to comment. But they printed the story anyway after VaRhonda let them read a letter you wrote to her talking about one of your checkups and how you weren't returning to work anytime soon. And the bitch recorded y'all conversation."

I held my head down in shame and let the tears fall. "I can't believe that," I said. "And I can't believe I'm here with her now!" I wiped the tears from my eyes. "Ooh, I'm gon' slap the hell outta that bitch!" I mumbled out loud.

I must've been louder than I thought because, as a young man was coming out of the men's restroom, he looked at me as if I was crazy.

Simone shook her head. "Chile, you know your days as a gold digger are over." She quickly checked the state of her acrylic nails.

I folded my arms across my chest. "Yeah, I'm sure. It just sucks that it took all of this for it to be over. It ain't have to end like this. I thought it would've ended when I got bored with it." I said as I thought about all the artists I had slept with and how they would read about my STD-story and throw dirt on my name after that. I wouldn't be surprised if they started opening up to tell their story about sleeping with me. This was bad, really bad.

"It can only get worse from here, huh?"

Simone replied, "No, girl. They might've got you down, but you ain't out! You take this experience and use it to stimulate your growth."

"But how am I gonna get back to my hustle, now that the music industry and its momma done found out about my chlamydia crisis?" I snapped. "It's a wrap."

"No," Simone rejected. "You can return to modeling, you can't return to sleeping around."

She frowned. "I kinda—well no, I did tell you the rules of a nasty game. But this new game I'm tryin'a put you on is the game I want to walk you through and be your lifeline along the way. Feel me?"

"I feel you, girl," I said. "But I appreciate it. Really, I do. Thanks."

"You just be thankful that you got another chance to make up for ya wrongs. I almost didn't!"

I wanted to ask her what she meant, but I left it alone for now.

Simone gave me a warm smile. She embraced me and took out her cell phone and told me to enter my number. "Now, I'm going back with my girls. I'll call you sometime this week. And take that VaRhonda cousin of yours home and handle her!"

I nodded and we departed ways.

Stranded

VaRhonda was shitty drunk by the time we left the club. I wasn't even tipsy! I did have a couple of men offer to buy me a drink finally, and I surprisingly declined. It was something about the talk with Simone that had me feeling different. After she gave me the real deal, I had no desire to sleep around or depend on a man for anything. This time it was more positive, as in "I am good enough to succeed in any and everything I do." *Well, maybe not everything; there are some things I'm just not cut out to do.*

VaRhonda was drifting off to sleep as soon as I strapped her seat belt on after helping her in the passenger seat. I walked around the Porsche to the other side and got into the driver's seat. I started up my car and checked out how I was doing on gas. The meter was right underneath full, giving me enough gas to go where I had to go.

I drove out of the parking lot and headed in the direction opposite from Queen Street. VaRhonda must have felt the direction of the car, because she woke up and asked where we were going.

"Girl, I got to get some gas for real cheap in the cut," I replied.

"The cut?" she asked, looking at my gas meter. "Bitch, you're right underneath full. What the fuck you need gas for?"

"Just go back to sleep," I said. "Why do you even care? You never cared about me!"

VaRhonda sucked her teeth. "Kirrah, what the fuck is you talking about?"

"Good night," I rejected her question.

When I was sure she was asleep, I ceased driving around the freeway and got on it. I took the 405 to the 5. I stayed on 5, as if I was going toward Sacramento. I reached my destination, a place called Los Banos, California. I rubbed my hands together in anticipation. It was payback time.

I shook VaRhonda out of her sleep. "VaRhonda, girl, wake up!" I shouted.

VaRhonda shook out of her sleep. "What the hell? What do you want?"

I answered, "I want to talk to you about something."

"What about?" she groaned.

"*Urban Life*," I replied.

That woke her up quickly. She jumped up and took off her seat belt to stretch, only making my job easier. "Listen, if you read about it, they approached me. I didn't want—"

"Shut that shit up! The fact is you opened up your mouth to the media. I have never done anything wrong to you," I said. "I might've said some foul shit in my head, but that's where it stayed, my head."

VaRhonda sighed and looked out the window. "Where the fuck is we? I thought you were going to get some gas in the cut?"

"Yeah, that's when I get back to Inglewood," I said.

"When *you* get back to Inglewood?" VaRhonda asked with confusion.

"C'mon, let's have a smoke," I suggested, taking a cigarette out of the glove compartment. I put the car in park, and easily took my feet off the brake. I got out of the car, leaving my door open. I walked around to her side and opened the door.

VaRhonda slowly got out of the car. I smoothly drew my fist back and flung it forward, right at her nose. Blood started gushing out, but I was in no position to stop fighting. I was so hurt about what she did to me, and even though I was going to pay her back, I still wouldn't feel complete. But this would do.

I cried painfully as I fought her. I had her laid out on the ground.

I took her cell phone out of her pocket and closed the passenger door. I got back into the car on the driver's side and turned my car around, heading back toward Inglewood.

Now that that was done, I could forget about VaRhonda until she found a ride from nowhere and was back in Inglewood. Hopefully, she could walk the road to the nearest city. If not, she was stranded.

Benny

After reaching Inglewood around seven in the morning, I went into my bedroom and collapsed on my bed to sleep. I was so tired, worn, and depressed. I wondered if what I'd just done to VaRhonda was the right thing. Revenge can only get you but so far.

It felt good when I did it, but three hours into the slow ride home, I began to reconsider my actions. I knew I would not turn back to get her because I didn't have the gas for that. I made it home damn near underneath empty and got my gas (as I said) from the gas station in the cut. Prices were the lowest I had seen them in months.

I wanted to call somebody and talk to them. There was no more VaRhonda to talk all my problems out with or brag to. Benny was no longer a part of my life. I never really confided in my mother and aunt, except about the chlamydia issue. Simone was probably asleep and would curse me out for calling so early in the morning.

Where's a friend when you need one? I browsed

through my phone caller ID looking for a familiar number. All down the line it was VaRhonda, Benny, Benny, Benny, Mom, Benny, Benny, Auntie, Mom, VaRhonda, Benny, Benny, Benny, Benny. I began crying when I realized the one person I used to depend on for everything had been shut out of my life because of my attitude. If I could take that back, I would do it in a heartbeat.

I wiped the tears from my eyes and pressed talk. I couldn't even keep the tears away for long. They came streaming down as I realized how sorry I was for treating someone I loved very much so wrong.

With tears in my eyes, I called Benny. I forced myself to stay awake even though I was mighty tired.

"Benny?" I sobbed after he picked up on the first ring.

"What's wrong, Kirrah?" he asked. He sounded relieved to hear from me even though it had only been a day.

"Yeah, it's me," I answered. "How are you, Benny?"

"Um, tired actually. You caught me in the middle of a dream, but it's okay." He chuckled.

I grinned.

"So, what brings you to call me?"

I sighed heavily and replied, "Benny, I heard some terrible things. I heard some really bad things and I am so hurt."

"What happened?"

"All I have to say is *Urban Life*," I replied.

"Oh, no," Benny said. "They approached me,

and I definitely declined their offer to speak! I didn't say anything! Not a word, Kirrah."

"I know it wasn't you," I cried. "It was VaRhonda."

"Your own cousin? Your own flesh and blood?" Benny shrieked. "That's crazy! Did you beat her ass?"

He made me laugh, in spite of all of my sadness. "Benny, you finally sound Black." I giggled. "Yeah, it was my cousin. I didn't even read the article. I went to the club and some other ladies told me about it. I couldn't believe she put me on blast like that. Didn't she know that if I wanted to open up about it, I would've told the magazines myself? Benny, I wanted to beat the shit out of her!"

"Did you?!"

"Yeah! All the way in Los Banos, California! And I left her ass stranded there!" I replied.

Benny cracked up with laughter. "Are you kidding me? How in the hell did that happen? Were you fighting in the car and just landed in Los Banos?"

I answered, "No, I drove there, got her out the car, then whupped her ass and left her there. I kinda feel bad, though."

"Revenge is sweet!" Benny said, as if he didn't hear the last sentence I said.

"This kind of revenge isn't," I answered.

"Well, what can you do? It already happened. No matter how sorry you feel, you still whipped her ass and stranded her!" Benny couldn't speak without laughing.

It brought me joy to hear him laugh. At least one of us was amused by this situation.

"I wonder how much money they paid her," I said.

Benny responded, "Believe me! As big as you are, they paid big bucks to know that. It contained drama and scandal, too?" Benny knew VaRhonda didn't leave out any details about my affairs with artists, at least the ones she knew about.

"As big as I *was*, you mean," I corrected.

"No, I stand uncorrected. You still are a star to me," Benny replied. "Kirrah, I didn't want to stop being your agent. In fact, if we can start over, I can get you onto bigger and better things than being in somebody's video."

"I have a new pursuit in life," I said.

I informed him about the BET experience I wanted to test out and told him some of my other goals, like becoming a TV personality or starting my own company.

I was glad to have Benny back, and I was sure he was glad to have me back. We made amends and planned to meet each other for dinner that night.

After we talked business, we went dancing. Benny wasn't the best dancer, but he could keep up. From then on, we developed a partnership and friendship that I wanted to keep around. Benny was one of those people who was so dedicated to a friend that it made you cry to know you were blessed with someone so wonderful.

This Is the Way . . .

The following Monday, Simone called me and told me to meet her at Cooley's Jamaican Restaurant on Crenshaw. I met her there for lunch. I ordered a Jamaican chicken patty and some curried goat and rice. She ordered jerk chicken wings and cabbage. We engaged in conversation as we waited for our food.

"So, how have you been over the past couple of days?" Simone asked before taking a sip of her Sprite.

"Good. I let a lot of things go, and a lot of people," I said, referring only to VaRhonda. "I gained some good friends back, and I'm ready for life to go in a new path."

"Girl, that's wassup!" Simone said. "I'm proud of you. That's how you bounce back. Don't let that shit get you down."

"Yeah," I cleared my throat. "Um, Simone, what did you mean when you said you've been where I am?"

Simone gave me an interesting look, looked down

at the table, and let a tear fall to the plate underneath her. "Well, Kirrah," she quivered, "I have been where you are."

"Meaning you had an STD?" I asked.

"Yes."

"Oh, that's okay. Why are you crying?" I asked, feeling relieved that there was someone I knew who had been in my position.

"Well, my issue was I can't just get rid of it as simply. It's a bit more complex. I only thank God I got it checked out just in time," Simone said.

"Well, what happened? What did you get?" I asked eagerly.

Simone choked up. She took a napkin and dabbed the corner of her eyes and wiped her nose. "I have hepatitis B. It completely changed my life forever."

"About a year and a half ago, I went to the doctor just in time. I was on my way to liver cancer, Kirrah. But I woke up one morning and something told me to go to the doctor. I didn't listen. I turned on the television and it was on the Discovery Health Channel and it was talking about STD's and shit. Then, I started reading *Ebony* magazine and there was an article about hepatitis B in women. I don't know what it was, but something was forcing me to go to the doctor," Simone said.

"That's crazy," I replied. "Are you better?"

"I just keep getting better over time, just like you keep getting prettier with age."

"Damn, I would never imagine you had Hep B," I said. "So you slipped up?"

"I didn't slip up. I made sure they had on a condom, but something escaped." She giggled. "I can laugh and joke about it now, but back then it was no laughing matter. You should've seen me. I seriously thought I was going to die."

"You better stay positive in the midst of all the negativity," I said.

"As long as you promise you'll do the same." she replied. "And we can't let no man get to us, no matter how good he looks. Deal?"

"Girl, that's a deal. I realized, can't no man do nothing for me in the long run. Kirrah has got to depend on Kirrah and Kirrah only."

"This is the way it should be!" Simone said.

"This is the way it's going to be," I corrected.

I gave her my word. The wind chimes on the door jingled as the finest Jamaican man walked into the restaurant. He walked past our table and tossed me a wink and a dazzling smile.

I looked at Simone. "I call him!"

Simone cracked up with laughter. "Girl, you better quit! He ain't been in the restaurant but five seconds and you already calling shotgun! How you know I didn't want the front-seat ride?"

"Ah, lawd," I laughed, remembering our pact. "This is going to be harder than I thought."

PART THREE:

$$ *Theori Cameron* $$

Theori Cameron

I was thrilled when I read my acceptance letter from University of California Los Angeles, abbreviation: UCLA. Who knew that a high-yella, green-eyed girl coming straight outta Compton would be getting into this highly acclaimed university? There was a time I didn't believe it could happen. I'll be the first to admit it too. I did deserve this; then again I didn't.

My days at Compton High School were rough. I was the source of envy for damn near all the females because of my undeniable beauty, and I wasn't cool, because I was considered a "geek" for being in the Honors program—Yes, there's an honors program at Compton High School!—Surprisingly, some of the girls befriended me, and we became a nice group of friends.

Right before winter break of my junior year, they jumped me without reason. I honestly believe it was their setup from the get-go. But I didn't let it faze me. I handled my own and got more involved in education, excelling in all subjects.

When senior year came around, I switched up the game and came to school with a whole new look, wearing clothes that showed off my curves and highlighted my figure. The thugs at school clung to me like crazy. I adored the attention and took in all the compliments to help my confidence. After a month of school, I became the boys' favorite homegirl.

Now, there were rumors about me fucking all the guys that I was cool with. That wasn't true yet. In fact, I remained a virgin until the spring break weekend of senior year. This boy named Jayshaun who graduated the year before had the privilege of being my first. It was good, it was rough, and it was addictive. It practically turned me into a freak. And that's when I steadily began having sex with some of the guys in my school. I was considered a ho, but truth of the matter was, that wasn't how I considered myself. I was just a girl getting her kicks in while she could, and those niggas loved it.

Females definitely hated it and were always up in my face, claiming I slept with their man. Hell, that wasn't my fault. I told them they better start tightening the leash on their men before I took the reigns . . . if I already hadn't.

I had to fight a couple of jealous bitches and whip their asses to show them I had put some of the summer into kickboxing classes. At first it was to tone my body in a fun way, but I realized with my good looks it would come in handy.

Now that I was a freshman at UCLA, those girls didn't matter. They were probably still in high school or somewhere chasing some nigga who couldn't do shit for them. I was the true winner. I graduated at the top of my high school class! My mom and dad were so proud, but became so sad when they broke the news to me that they were moving to North Carolina over the summer. The worst thing about the news was receiving it on my graduation day. The only reason they didn't move sooner was because they wanted me to finish up my senior year at Compton High School and get into UCLA.

They felt ready enough to let me face the city alone. They got the hell up out of Compton and purchased a home in North Carolina. The agreement was a solid three hundred a month for college and my expenses. Six hundred was all I could receive from them. After all, we were not rich. My parents were not financially secure enough to take out a loan and bear the consequences of its high interest rate. Even with my grants, my education and living was burning a hole through my wallet. I was struggling to pay for my apartment, my UCLA tuition, and my personal expenses. I had an eviction notice ready to be posted on my door.

I begged Mommy and Daddy to spare me some more money. Thank God they did. That, unfortunately, went on for a couple of months. I got the call from Mommy saying they couldn't give me any money anymore and I would have to get a job. The money stopped coming in.

Not wanting to harass them about it, I made the ultimate sacrifice and dropped out of UCLA. It was too expensive. I vowed to return in the future, but right now, it was impossible. But I still wanted to get an education. I put myself in a more affordable college . . . a junior college . . . Compton Community College. That way, I was able to stay in school and not worry about burning my wallet.

There was one problem. I still hadn't gotten a job, and the last of my money in the bank was going on empty. Now, in my high school days, I took a stab at working fast food. I could not take it. The smell of the fast food made me nauseous. I tried retail, but was quickly fired because I didn't know how to handle the rude customers in a ladylike manner. I tried working at a day care, and I quickly came to the conclusion that I didn't want any kids. In fact, I could not stand any job I took.

One of my homies told me to try stripping. I looked good, had a banging body, I could dance, and I was flexible. So I said, "Hell, why not?"

Compton's Eye Candy

Confident in my physical appearance, face and body, I drove my old bucket to Eye Candy, a strip club on Compton Boulevard. I decided to ask for work there and hoped that my looks would guarantee me a job. I pulled into the parking lot and parked my car. When I got to the doors of the strip club, I asked the bodyguard if I could speak to the owner about a job. He looked me up and down as if he was inspecting to see if I was Eye Candy quality. He paged a second bodyguard to assist me.

Bodyguard number two took me into the strip club and led me toward the back rooms. He took me down a hall and led me to the owner's office. I was then introduced to Luther "Crook" Robinson, the owner of Eye Candy.

He was around fifty-something with shades covering his eyes and relaxed hair. Age was reflected on his worn skin. He dressed crisp and clean, like an old-time pimp or hustler. Crook waved bodyguard number two off. I sat down in the chair in front of his desk nervously. Crook waited for bodyguard number two to close the door before speaking. I felt like I was in the hot seat for something I sure as hell did.

Once I heard Crook's smooth, mellow voice, a lot of the tension left my body.

"What's your name, baby doll?" he asked.

"Theori Cameron," I answered.

"No, baby doll, stage name," he replied.

I shook my head, embarrassed. "Um, no, sorry. I don't have one yet," I said, adding a friendly smile.

He nodded approvingly, glad to be the one who would give me my stage name. "Stand up," he commanded.

I stood up.

"Can you lose some of those clothes?" he asked.

"You want me to dance or just take them off?" I asked.

"I'm just checking out your body to see if you are what Eye Candy is looking for. You know I only want the females with the baddest bodies in Compton. A lot of females come in my office looking for a job. If they don't got it, then they can't flaunt it, at least not here."

I laughed. I knew I had it, and now I definitely wasn't scared. I took off my clothes and remained in my push-up bra from Victoria's Secret and my G-string. I watched his eyes glance at my 36Cs and follow my curves down to my ankles.

He told me to turn around. I turned around and felt his eyes staring at my smooth, round ass. He cleared his throat and I began putting my clothes back on.

"Redbone," he said. He took a sip of his strong brandy, in his clear pimp cup.

"Excuse me?" I asked for my own clarification.

"Redbone is your new stage name. That's a light-skin, thick chick. That's what they call 'em down South. I think it suits you," he explained.

I nodded. Redbone was cute for a nickname and it would have to do. "So does this mean I got the job?" I asked, sitting back down in the chair.

"Oh, hell yeah!" Crook said. "I've been waiting for a sexy female like yourself to be added to my club. I just put another girl on the lineup about two days ago."

He took out some papers, and we went over the rules and regulations of the club. I understood totally and told him I was only there to make my cash, not friends or relationships. Just the cash. Crook and I shook hands and thus began my job as a stripper.

Crook scheduled me to work that Friday night. My first night at Eye Candy would hopefully be beneficial, talking in a financial sense. I waited backstage for the DJ to introduce me.

"And now presenting to all players, haters, gangbangers and perpetrators . . . the light-skin, thick chick—Redbone!"

I sashayed out on stage and over to the pole. I grabbed the pole and danced around it. I wasn't ready to swing. I had not learned how to do that yet. I be damned if I was gonna fall and bust my ass in front of these men. Boy, did I put on a show! I was so tantalizing in my red bustier and blue satin bow V-string.

My first ten was placed around my V-string. I

dipped low to the floor, rolled over, and dropped into a split. The men immediately started hollering and tossing bills my way. I snatched them up and stuffed them in any available place on my body, whether it was my bra or V-string. They slapped bills on me, and I gladly took them. I had them right where I wanted them: screaming for me!

I looked at them seductively, making eye contact with a select few who seemed the most helpless. I let them catch a quick stare into my green eyes and then looked away.

"Oh, I'll be back for some more gentlemen." I laughed as I walked off the stage. My music was almost over.

They cheered me off. Some were upset, however, because they wanted to see more of me.

"I know that's right!" one of the girls said to me when I came backstage.

"Thanks, girl," I said as I began counting my money. I was by no means trying to make friends. Plus, I knew if I became friends with these girls, that would only mean drama. I saw the movie *Player's Club*. Bitches were foul! At that moment in my life, money was my homie.

"How much you make?" she asked.

I shrugged nonchalantly. "I don't know."

"My name is Inez, but at the club they call me Mickey," she answered.

I wanted to snicker. "Why Mickey?" I asked, holding in my laughter.

"'Cuz of this," she turned around, lifted up her mini satin skirt and showed me the tattoo of a thugged-out Mickey Mouse on her left ass cheek.

"How long you been working here?"

"This is my first night, and I'm nervous as hell!" she replied. "I don't want to get shot if I ain't appealing to these niggas."

I laughed. "Chill out, ma. All of them are drunk and about one drink away from passing out. I wonder why Crook doesn't want us to go out there and entertain until the DJ calls us all out."

"That nigga just tryin'a be different, that's what I think. Usually the strippers can go out and work the audience while another one is on stage. Crook wants to run things his way. What kind of strip club has sofas and couches instead of the regular tables? He's tryin'a be luxurious. Girl, the VIP room is like a whole 'nother club. Flat-screen TVs of the bitch who's doing her thang onstage! What in the world? I'm surprised ain't nobody try to steal that shit," Mickey replied. "That's cool, though. Being different makes you stand out. And everybody knows about Eye Candy."

She lit a cigarette, but didn't have time to smoke it. One of the girls came in and said that it was time for her to go on stage. She left out to do her thing.

Later on in the night, the DJ announced for all nine girls at Eye Candy to come on to the stage. I got out there and searched for the guy who seemed to be ballin' the most. I figured he would be in VIP popping his own bottle of bubbly. I went to the VIP and gave a lap dance to one of the top-notch thugs in there. He pulled out a wad of hundreds. I was able to work six hundred out of him. I was fortunate enough to land a dance with his fine ass.

Damn, I thought, *I hope he comes often.* I memorized his face, so I would be able to spot him next next time he came back to the club. His entourage blessed me with some bills as well, but they didn't have my interest. I looked at the dude I was dancing on. I scanned his many tattoos. There was a tattoo on his arm that said: LPP "KILLA MARK."

"You betta come and see me again, baby," I said in his ear. I gave it a quick lick and walked away.

I found it strange that right before closing the strip club for the night, Crook asked to speak to Mickey and me. We entered his office and wondered what in the hell was going on. Why were we the only two strippers who were asked to speak to him? Was it because this was our first night?

"How long y'all two been working here?" Crook asked.

"It's my first night," Mickey answered.

"Mine too," I added.

Crook nodded his head and said, "Exactly. So why are y'all acting like the veterans of this muthafucka? Didn't I tell you that three strippers are assigned to work the floor on different nights? It wasn't y'all turn to work the damn floor! You shoulda stayed y'all asses onstage!"

"What are you talking about?" I asked, trying my damn hardest not to get an attitude. Crook was acting like he was our daddy or some shit. Not even my daddy talked to me like that!

"When we called for all the ladies to come to the stage, you two were the only bitches to go into the damn audience. We already had three strippers working the floor. Who told y'all to do that?" Crook asked angrily.

I looked at Mickey and she shrugged her shoulders. "Nobody did, Crook," she answered with a pinch of attitude.

Crook continued, "Redbone, your ass is in VIP, and Mickey, you down in the center taking all eyes off of the damn stage! Some of these bitches made little or no money! And that hurts me and my pockets, damn it!"

I smirked. I took some money out of my jacket pocket, which was supposed to be my share. I handed Crook four hundred dollars. "Will this show for our apologies?"

Crook snatched the money up greedily. "Hmm, yes, it would. But this is a warning, so don't do it again. Now this is a heads-up: The other ladies are starting to talk."

Mickey and I apologized once more. We agreed we would not do that without his permission. The next thing to come out of Mickey's mouth surprised me, but was also enlightening.

"Well, peep this, Crook," she began. "How about you just let Redbone and I get our own duet performance whenever we come in together? We're obviously two of the finest strippers here and also the most hated."

Crook smiled and asked, "Y'all tryin'a play me?"

"No, no. She's right," I said. "You'll have those men lined up around the building to see our performance!" I put my arm around Mickey.

Crook said, "Y'all be here on time tomorrow and we'll see how it goes, alright?"

Mickey and I nodded and left his office. I gave her props for coming up with that suggestion. I recognized how the other girls were already operating. They already hated me, well, Mickey and me, just because we were trying to get our paper. I thought the drama started when I did make friends. But I realized that wasn't the case. Mickey was, so far, a cool-ass chick. Game recognized game, and she and I had the same game plan. I decided to allow myself to have one friend . . . and that was Mickey.

Redbone and Mickey

". . . Y'all betta get out ya wallets 'cuz this ain't no free show! Redbone and Mickey are gonna let you know!" the DJ said as he put on Compton native rapper, The Game's "Let's Ride."

Mickey and I came out and performed, and took every dollar bill we saw. Those guys were ours when we began dancing together, giving them a girl-on-girl peep show. They were anxious to see us go further. The lights went out right when we would lean in to kiss, all part of our act. When the lights came back on, we were offstage. Mickey and I never got it twisted, this was NO LESBO! It was just an act for the money. We liked the attention we got, and loved the money we made.

Crook worshipped the ground we walked on for bringing more attention to Eye Candy. Week after week, more guys came to the club to check out our duo performance. People as far as West Covina would come to the controversial city of Compton to check out Eye Candy because of a he-said/she-said, "Redbone and Mickey are two of the finest strippers working!"

The other strippers were ready to beat our asses because we were the talk of the club. They would have to get over it. If they didn't like it, there were other strip clubs all over South Central that could use them. Mickey and I could hold it down at Eye Candy.

One night after Mickey and I performed, we were sitting at the giant vanity mirror we asked Crook for, talking about why we started stripping.

"I ain't even gonna lie," Mickey began. "I love the attention. Shit, I was one of the flyyest bitches at Centennial High and bitches hated it! I'm not going to college, and I need to do something so I won't have to settle for nothing. I'm gonna do something I enjoy, sheeit! I can hang with the strip thing 'cuz when I was a senior I used to do it at the hood parties for all my gangbanging friends. My mom was a stripper, my grandma was too."

"Girl, I needed some money to pay for college because all of sudden my parents in North Carolina couldn't send me my six hundred dollars a month. How fucked-up is that? I was at UCLA, but I didn't have the funds to stay there. So now I'm at Compton Community College, working here at Eye Candy."

"Well, well, well," said Tasty, one of the jealous strippers. She walked over toward us with two other women behind her. "If it ain't these two light-skinned heffas."

"Thinkin' they all of that," the second woman said.

"Y'all bitches got five seconds to get from behind me or else," Mickey threatened, eyeing them through the mirror.

"Or else what?" Tasty asked, leaning over us.

"Or else I'm gon' whup your old ass," Mickey threatened.

"And I'ma help!" I added.

"Bitch, I wish you would!" Tasty said, getting loud.

"You wish I would?" Mickey repeated. She was stunned that Tasty was actually trying to step to her. Mickey was crazy, and would give Tasty exactly what she was asking for, whup-ass of a lifetime.

I looked at Mickey and said, "These hoes don't even know."

"Make me know then!" Tasty snickered, slightly pushing us.

The push didn't faze me at all. It wasn't even intimidating. Before I could grab Mickey to tell her these women were not even worth it, she was throwing punches at Tasty. I tried to pull Mickey away from her.

One of the girls doomed herself when she hit me. I began fighting her. It was Mickey and I against these three jealous broads. I was surprised none of the other haters jumped in to aid them.

One of the security guards came in and broke it up. He pulled Mickey and me away from the girls.

"All of you, in Crook's office now!" he yelled.

We marched into Crook's office and waited to hear what came next.

"What the hell happened?" Crook asked. He had much anger in his voice and an even angrier look on his face. "Tasty?"

"Mickey just started hitting me, baby," she said in a sweet, innocent voice.

Crook looked at Mickey for an explanation.

She simply said, "That bitch pushed me first."

"Nah, Mickey attacked us first," the women said. "I swear to you, Crook!"

"Ah, hell nah! Why are y'all lying?" I asked angrily. "You approached us first!"

"ENOUGH!" Crook yelled. "I know how to handle this. Excuse me for a minute while I watch the security tape."

Crook went into a second room where the TVs were. Crook had security cameras installed in the club for safety reasons.

He came back and sat down in his chair. "Mickey, you did swing on her first," he said calmly.

"Did you see her push us first?" Mickey said.

"Well," Crook said. "Yes, but it wasn't too violently. You shoulda talked to me when she pushed you, Mickey."

"Well, ain't this a bitch!" Mickey sucked her teeth and folded her arms.

"You ain't off the hook either, Redbone. I clearly saw you fighting them too," Crook informed.

I rolled my eyes. "Which means you clearly saw them fighting us, right? I sure did swing on them bitches because one of them hoes hit me!" I pointed to the two girls. "They musta been crazy to think I wasn't gonna fight back! Bitch must be crazy."

"Have you two read the rules?" Crook asked. "Y'all know physical alt-alta . . . um . . . alteruh . . . altercations are not tolerated here at Eye Candy."

"Man, fuck the rules! We live in the city of fucking Compton! Fighting is a part of life!" Mickey yelled. "And stop trying to use big words!"

Mickey and I snickered, pissing Crook off even more.

"You guys can't be fighting all up and through here! I have to enforce the rules," Crook said.

I asked, "Does *y'all* include Tasty and them other hoes?'

"Yes, it does!" Crook said. "Tasty, Peachy, and Delicious have two weeks suspension. Redbone and Mickey have a month."

Mickey and I looked at each other. We were shocked at this unfair bullshit.

"What the fuck? No, no! Why do we have a damn month?" Mickey asked, banging her hand on the desk.

Crook opened his mouth to speak, but I cut him off.

"Don't even answer that question. You don't have to worry about Mickey and I coming back. We fucking quit!" I yelled. "Mickey, let's go!"

"Now wait a fucking minute!" Crook yelled. "You're quitting me? Over the rules I made? Are you bitches crazy?"

"*You* must be crazy to think we're going to work for a fool like you. Your ass couldn't even see these bitches provoked the fight and it was on fucking tape. I hope Tasty sucks one hell of a dick, because it just cost you two of your best strippers!" I responded angrily.

"Hold on, damn it! I make the rules! Didn't none of you bitches open up Eye Candy! I did! I opened up Eye Candy! Whatever I say goes! You heard me, bitches?" Crook yelled.

Whatever Crook was saying fell on deaf ears. His unfair ways made him lose two good strippers. I realized I was better off working elsewhere than with a shady muthafucker like Crook. If he was already acting foolishly and I hadn't even been there six months, then I knew the worst was yet to come.

I left the room with Mickey hot on my trail. She was unsure about the decision I had made for us.

"Girl, you do realize we're out of a job, Redbone!" Mickey said.

"I know, girl, but it's all good," I promised. "We gon' get our paper, believe that!"

Theori and Inez

For the next month, I was out of luck, and Inez was out of a home. She had missed her rent and the landlord had zero tolerance for that kind of shit. The next week, she was evicted and looking for a spot. I welcomed her into my apartment. This would hopefully be a good thing in the future, meaning we would go half and half on rent . . . once we had a job again.

Shit got complicated as hell. I was fearful of the future because my shit looked grim. I figured that in a cool month or so, I'd be homeless too. I didn't know what kind of patience my landlord had.

I made the decision to go to my number one source, and my boyfriend from way back in the day, Jayshaun. I had been getting some money out of him for two weeks now. I was doing all of this without even having to give him some pussy. I was practicing abstinence and was surprising even my damn self at how well I was doing. It had been about nine months since I'd last had sex.

Today I was once again in the need of some money and gave Jayshaun a call.

"Jayshaun, baby. Can you loan me some money?" I cooed when he answered the phone. "Please, baby?"

"Theori, what the fuck are you talking 'bout? I gave your ass five hundred fucking dollars last week. How you spend that shit already?" Jayshaun asked, anger rising in his voice.

"I had to pay the phone bill, boo. And you do want me to keep my phone on so you can call me, right?" I asked. I looked at Inez and rolled my eyes from doing this every-other-day routine.

"What am I gonna get in return?" Jayshaun asked.

Today would be the day he asks what's in it for him. "Jayshaun, what do you mean? You got me, babe."

"I ain't talking about that and you know it," Jayshaun replied. "I been letting you slide just 'cuz I got love for you. But you can't always expect something for nothing. I'm gon' tell you straight up. The next time you want something from me, you gotta give me something."

"Something like what?" I asked, playing dumb again.

"Some head or some pussy. Hell, get creative with it," Jayshaun snickered.

I sucked my teeth. "So you gon' front me the money or what?"

"Yeah, I got you. Just pick it up later on in the week," Jayshaun told me.

I got off the phone with him and looked at Inez, scribbling in her notepad. She had been working on a novel for the past year. I had read bits and pieces of it and was waiting for her to complete it. It was interesting and intriguing.

"The girl has long wet-looking brown hair, fair skin, with sparkling brown eyes. The 36Ds she has are tantalizing. They flatter her twenty-six-inch waist and thirty-six-inch hips. Being a mixed breed of Creole, African-American and Mexican, she is every man in the hood's dream girl," Inez read. "You like it, girl?"

It seemed as if she was describing herself. "Sounds like a bestseller already," I complimented. "Sure wish you'd finish it and get it published so we can have some money."

"I know, right?" Inez agreed. "We don't know where next month's rent is coming from. We don't know how we're going to get groceries. Hell, we don't know nothing!"

"You telling me! Jayshaun said he ain't giving me no more money without some pussy. I have been getting this free ride for two weeks now. His patience is already low," I said. "But his hormones are high. That nigga is a walking dick!"

"What the hell are we gonna do?" Inez asked. "It sucks to be broke."

"Girl, we doing all right though. We got an apartment on Rosecrans Avenue and Long Beach Boulevard! We're trying to survive in the city of Compton. We look damn good too!"

"I'll smoke to that," Inez said. "But I'm too broke to buy weed!"

I laughed at her. The idea I had for us hit me in my brain so suddenly, it was scary. I ran to the sofa and sat next to Inez. I grabbed her hands. "Girl, why do I have the best idea for us ever?!" I exclaimed.

"What is it?" Inez said, almost freaking out.

"You know how you used to strip at them parties? Why don't we do the same thing?" I asked.

"Say what?" Inez asked.

"You know the gangbangers like throwing those functions and get-togethers every once in a while—"

"More like every other week," Inez cut me off.

"Yeah," I agreed. "You know they have that paper too. We can go to the parties and dance there. We'll charge a down payment of five hundred dollars for our services."

"Kinda like private-party strippers," Inez clarified.

I nodded my head. "And we'll just be Theori and Inez. Fuck that nickname shit! All the niggas in Compton will be begging for us to come turn they party out, no matter what hood!"

Inez bit her bottom lip, a gesture that I had never seen before.

"Girl, what are you thinking?"

"I'm thinking you got a plan! Theori, I got to give it to you. That's what's up. As a matter of fact, I'ma holla at the homies and see what's good with this weekend."

"Do that, girl. Check it out, we gon' go to the party just dressed like normal. We ain't getting all fancy and shit," I said.

Inez nodded. "Girl, this is gon' be like working a bachelor party every week!" She giggled and got on the phone to book us our first gig.

It's a Bompton Mob Piru Thang

"Girl, where did Big Ty say this party was at?" I asked Inez as we rolled down the streets of Compton looking for the correct address.

"On Rosecrans and Willowbrook. I think we shoulda made a left back there," Inez said. "You shoulda known that already. Girl, we about to be running the streets of Compton."

"All right, let me turn around," I said, making an illegal U-turn at the light. "I hope they ain't gon' be mad at us for being late."

"Big Ty won't, but his boys probably will," Inez admitted. "Let's just hurry up, get there, and make this money."

We made it to the party and were greeted by gangsta rap, weed, and a rough gang of Compton Bloods from the Bompton Mob Pirus. Most were laced in all-black with burgundy bandanas. All eyes were on us when we made our way through the party.

"Damn, what the fuck took y'all bitches so damn

long?" one of Big Ty's drunken homies yelled as we entered the party.

I wondered if Inez realized we were two of the only five girls in the place. I was scared out of my mind of these guys. I wasn't even gonna front. I wasn't trying to do anything wrong tonight because I thought it would be my ass if I fucked up. All I wanted to do was dance for them and get the hell out of Dodge.

"Put on some real music," Inez told Big Ty.

He put on something fast for us to dance to. I felt the faster the music, the quicker I could strip and get my ass up out of there. Inez and I immediately stripped down to our lingerie and began working the living room and everyone in it.

It wasn't as safe as working in the strip club. First of all, there wasn't a bodyguard to stop these guys from grabbing us. Secondly, most of them were drunk out of their minds and horny as hell. Third, damn near everybody was strapped for the occasion. Anything could happen to me and Inez. We were willing to take the risk just for some cash.

Inez had the left side of the room, and I had the right. I sat on laps and grinded on dicks while I caught bills with my mouth and free hand. I pulled their bandanas and placed it in between my legs to show them I had love for Pirus. Inez bent over and let the Mickey Mouse on her ass be slapped repeated times with bills. She would get in between two dudes and take each bill they had. We made more money than we did at the strip club, and didn't have to turn it in to no Crook.

The night was over for us when there were no

more bills for us to collect. Either we took everything they had, or they were stingy with the cash
hiding in their pockets. We told the gentlemen
we'd see them around and to holla at Big Ty if they
were throwing another party.

Inez and I went home in one piece and full of
happiness. This was it. We entered the apartment
and took our earnings, and I do mean *earnings*, to
our bed to count it. We were thrilled when we saw
we had reached a little over eighteen hundred dollars. Not bad for our first night.

"Ooh, this call for a celebration. Spark this shit
up," Inez said, taking a blunt out of her jacket
pocket.

"Where did you get that?" I asked her, looking at
the blunt in amazement.

"Big Ty gave it to me. He said he ain't have no
more money to give me, so he gave this to me as a
thank-you note," she laughed as she put in Bone
Thugs-n-Harmony's CD.

"Foe Tha Love of $" with Eazy-E came on, and I
nodded my head as I lit the blunt with my lighter.

Inez danced over to the bed after turning the
stereo up a few notches.

I passed her the fat blunt and watched her take
a hit. She lifted her head and blew the smoke toward the ceiling. Her next puff she inhaled and
breathed out of her nose.

"Perfect song on! A bitch on this tip all for the
love of money. I got a feeling I ain't gon' be able to
stop this shit!"

"You ain't never lie!" I said, lying down on my
bed. I ran my hand through the bills on the bed. I

wanted to do what the super rich people do on cartoons and just throw the money up in the air, but I was in no mood to re-gather it from around the room. I felt satisfied and wasn't afraid of the future, for once.

The phone rang and shook me out of my comfortable thoughts. I handed the blunt to Inez, and she began to dance gracefully to the gangsta groove of Bone Thugs-n-Harmony.

I answered the phone. "What up?"

"Theori?" Jayshaun's raspy voice was so noticeable.

"Hey, baby," I said as the buzz from the weed started to kick in.

"Theori, what up with you? You ain't stopped by to get the money?" Jayshaun turned his Alpine car system down. The bass was overriding my voice.

"Ah, nah, Jayshaun. I don't need your money no more. I got a job," I said with a giggle. "But thank you anyway, baby."

"Well, since you got a job, why don't you pay me back?" Jayshaun snapped.

I laughed and hung up in his face. Jayshaun was no longer needed. I wouldn't have to depend on anybody, and that's what I wanted to feel . . . independence. After our financial success, Inez and I knew we'd be doing this more often. We had found our niche, our forte, our hustle.

South Side Compton

Crips

Istood silently in the shower washing my body with some Victoria's Secret shower gel and a sponge towel. I wiped away the sleep crust from my eyes and yawned dramatically. I don't know how far into the early morning Inez and I went to sleep. All I knew was I was paying for it right now. I could barely stand in the shower with my eyes open.

Inez and I had gone clubbing and had so much fun. She had become the sister I never dreamed I'd have. I smiled at the fact that it was like fate how we met up and how we clicked so fast. Another thing that put a smile on my face was the success of last week's Bompton Mob Piru party and the look on those guys' faces. I was pretty damn sure that somehow and some kind of way, word had spread to other hoods in Compton. It was only a matter of time before calls started coming in.

I got out the shower, washed my face, and brushed my teeth. With a towel wrapped around my body, I exited the bathroom and walked toward my bedroom closet to find something to wear. I noticed the time as I walked past my night-stand. It was two in the afternoon and Inez was still knocked out. The phone rang eerily, causing me to jump at the interruption of silence.

"Hello?" I asked when I answered the telephone.

"Yeah, can I speak to Theori or Inez?" the male voice asked.

"This is Theori. Who is this?" I asked.

"Yo, this is Kentrell. Y'all working tonight or what? 'Cuz South Side Compton Crips is having a li'l party and I was tryin'a get y'all to come dance for me and my niggas," he said, stating his hood like he was banging on me or something.

"Oh," I said with a giggle. "Well, lucky for you, Inez and I ain't booked tonight. We can come. There's going to be a five-hundred-dollar deposit. Where's this shit at again?"

Kentrell gave me the information and directions. He added, "And you know this a South Side Compton event, so if you bringing some dudes from another hood it's a wrap." He hung up.

No, this rude-ass muthafucka didn't, I thought.

I went into the room to tell Inez the news. She was still in our bed sleep. I shook her out of it and waited for her to rub her eyes and sit up to hear what I had to say. "Party tonight on Pearl Avenue near South Park," I said, walking over to the other side of the room to open up the blinds.

"Damn," she yawned. "We picking up already! First week was Pirus and now it's South Side." She already knew the hood that was throwing this party just from where it was located.

"And next week it'll be another party. Shit, this is what we chose to do. It's all about the paper," I replied.

That evening, Inez and I got ready for the party. We wanted to get there early so the boys from South Side Compton Crip wouldn't be mad. Thankfully, Kentrell gave me thorough directions.

We got to the party on time and realized we weren't the only females dancing for the guys tonight. Inez and I looked at each other and were offended. Our hustle wasn't one to be shared with any others.

"It's like ten other bitches here," Inez said, folding her arms. "We might as well be back at Eye Candy!"

"Them bitches are not cute, and they're wack. Inez, let's just go up in there and show them how it's done," I said.

That's exactly what Inez and I did. We went up in the room and took control. We commanded the atmosphere and made this performance all about us. We used moves that hadn't been used since the Eye Candy days. The men loved it and started tossing bills at us instead of the raggedy-ass bitches we had shown up.

"Oh shit, damn, this ho got ass!"

"Aye, shake dat shit, bitch!"

"Make it clap again!"

The things they shouted out were demeaning, but it let us know that they loved our performance.

One girl had to get stupid and literally move us out of the way so she could get attention, but the money had already been made. By this time, the men only wanted a show.

"I know this girl ain't tryin'a battle," I said in Inez's ear.

"Hell yeah, she is," Inez said.

Without consulting me about it, Inez went in for the kill and started dancing her ass off. The guys began hooting and hollering for her.

She beckoned me over, and I joined in. We danced our asses off and watched the other females stare at us in envy. Later on, they left the party because we had stolen their act. It wasn't anything new. Inez and I had been down that route before with the broads at Eye Candy.

A young attractive man with the letters SSCC tattooed across his chest came and put his arm around Inez and I. "These is my bitches, niggas!" he slurred his words.

Inez and I laughed at him.

"Kentrell, sit yo' drunk ass down!" a man yelled from the crowd. "We wanna see the hoes dance!"

"Well, y'all betta pull out some more cash! This ain't no free show, niggas!" brave Inez instructed them.

The things a man won't do for a sexy pair of women! These men took out more cash to see us continue on with the tease.

Overall, the South Side Compton Crips party was a memorable one. Inez and I left that party being the talk of the night, and with almost ten grand in our hands. However, we were soon going to realize that not all parties were going to be this fun.

Palmer Blocc
Compton Crips

The success of only two weeks and two parties allowed me and Inez to lay low and chill for the next couple of weeks. The rent was paid for the next three months, the bills were also paid in full. We could finally fix our jacked-up credit. Seriously, dancing at the hood parties was the best thing to happen to us.

Me and Inez's friendship grew tighter, upgrading us from friends, to best friends, to damn near sisters. I was introduced to her family, who resided in San Jose, with the exception of a few cousins in Lynwood, right next door to Compton.

Inez's cousin, Kilo, was a Crip from Palmer Blocc. He had lived in Lynwood all his life, but after graduating from Lynwood High School, he relocated to the west side of Compton on Willowbrook Avenue and West Compton Boulevard. A few weeks later, he got put on Palmer Blocc Compton Crips. Inez never forgot the day she was at her aunt's house and he came through the front door with a bruised face and a bloody mouth. Inez asked what happened and Kilo told her he fought his way through twelve dudes to get initiated into Palmer Blocc.

Kilo's best friend Darius was turning nineteen in a couple of days. He had heard of our little business and talked Inez and I into stripping for the birthday party. The party would be held at a friend's house on West Arbutus Street and Aranbe Avenue. Kilo ensured Darius that this party wouldn't be crashed by any gang fights.

Darius wasn't into gang activities. He was only living in Compton by force, not by choice. He was taking care of his sick, elderly mother and they didn't have the money to get the hell up out of Compton. Darius had big plans, though. He was studying business marketing at El Camino College. After he graduated with an AA degree, he would go on to a university to further his education. Darius just wanted to enjoy his birthday party, even if that meant all of his Crip banging friends had to be there.

We got to the party and were escorted to a bedroom where we could change. Inez had noticed that some of the guys in the room were some of the boys she had messed around with in her previous days.

"I feel more comfortable at this party because Kilo and his friends are here. Them niggas would never let shit happen to me. Not with me looking this good," she said, taking her pants off.

I nodded and stripped out of my shirt, revealing my breasts in a peek-a-boo bra. "That last party was crazy, but it was fun as hell. I hope this one can top that!" I did a quick mirror check.

"You look good," Inez said, opening the bedroom door.

"So do you," I replied, following her out of the room.

We walked out the bedroom, ready to get this party started and make this money.

"Y'all been waiting to see me?" I asked as Inez and I walked into the room half-naked.

The response was a cheer of "Oohs", "Hell Yeahs," and "Aw, Shits!"

Inez and I began dancing. Money was coming from all angles. Bills were being placed in our bras and thongs.

"Where's the birthday boy?" I asked seductively.

"Aw, shit!" Kilo exclaimed, slapping Darius on the back.

He brought him over to me and sat down on the sofa to watch.

Inez kept entertaining the crowd, and I personally entertained Darius. He didn't get overly excited. In fact, he was calm—too calm. I called Inez over to us, hoping that would hype him up a little bit. She sashayed over and joined in. She had him from the back, and I had him from the front. He seemed to be in his own world as we danced on him. If it weren't for the hard-on underneath his Dickies, I would've thought he was bored, or gay.

He didn't disrespect us by calling us out of our name or getting all touchy-feely. He just stood there and let us grind all over him. In my mind, I thanked him for being a gentleman and respecting us.

POP . . . POP . . . POP . . . POP!

"Cedar Block Piru, blood!"

POP . . . POP . . . POP!
"Fuck Palmer Blocc!"
POP!
The women screamed and dropped to the floor.
The men who were armed took out their guns and
began firing at the Pirus from Cedar Block at the
front door. At this point, I was crawling on the
floor looking for Inez. Several more shots were
fired before the Pirus ran off and the Palmer Blocc
Crips ran out the house. The continuous screams
of men and women horrified me.

"Ay, c'mon, Tre! Let's go! It's going down tonight, nigga! Get the heat for them bitches!" a
young and rowdy man yelled as he paced around
the room with a nine in his hand.

His boys nodded their heads. It was war now.
The Pirus from Cedar Block had came and shot up
the party, and they had to take care of business.
Everyone knew it was risky throwing a Crip party
so close to Pirus. Cedar Block Pirus' neighborhood was north of Palmer Blocc's territory. They
were the closet Blood and Crip rivals in this
neighborhood. They pulled a daring move cross-
ing over West Arbutus Street and coming onto
Palmer Blocc Crip's turf. Now the shootout would
result in a night of mayhem, a week of terror, and
a period of death, if things got fatal.

"Jamie? Baby, where are you?" a lady cried.

"Has anyone seen my li'l brotha?" a boy yelled
swinging his gun in the air.

"Ay 'cuz, you covered in blood!" a man hollered
when seeing his friend walk up to him. "You shot!"

His friend replied, "Nah, I'm okay. It ain't my
blood."

Somebody was shot. Somebody was dead. Somebody was scared. Somebody was still shooting. The gunshots crackled and echoed outside the house.

The police sirens were heard moments later, as if someone had flipped a switch and turned them on.

I was still on the floor, letting the helpless tears flow from my eyes.

"Darius," Kilo yelled. "C'mon, man! Stop playing! Wake up, man!"

"KILO!" Inez screamed. She crawled over to Kilo, who was holding Darius' bloody body.

"Inez!" I yelled, moving toward her as quickly as possible.

"Is he dead?" Inez asked.

Kilo leaned over his face and said, "Nah, not yet. He's still breathing." He then took out his cell phone and called for an ambulance.

"Is he gonna make it?" Inez wiped the tears from her eyes with the back of her hand.

"Sheeit, I don't know," mumbled an on-the-verge-of-crying Kilo. He tried his hardest not to break down in tears. "Darius, c'mon, man. C'mon, man. C'mon, man."

Seeing Kilo mourn for his best friend made me so sad that I felt sick, and seeing all the blood made me nauseous. I looked at Inez who had just wiped a tear away from her eye.

A helicopter flew over the house.

"Inez, Theori, go get yo' shit and leave. Go home now!" Kilo instructed.

"Kilo, please call me when you get home," Inez said. "Promise me now."

Kilo promised to call her and made us leave the house immediately. We went into the bedroom and grabbed our things and shook. We reached our apartment safe and sound. We went straight to our bed and went to sleep, trying to pretend everything that just happened did not.

Jayshaun Returns

The whole shootout on the west side of Compton had many people shaken up. It certainly had Inez and I ready to stay in the house and hide. We woke up and proceeded to count the previous night's earnings. It was a measly three hundred dollars. Surely we were tossed much more money than that, but when the shootout occurred we left the majority of that money on the floor. We only had what was tucked into our thongs—a few bills of ones, fives, tens and twenties.

Kilo did call Inez around four in the morning and informed us that Darius died on the way to the hospital. Two other people were injured.

"I can't believe he died, girl," I said, sick to my stomach of how shit went down the night before.

Inez nodded. "That's fucked-up. He was the only person in there who wasn't involved in gangs, and the only person to get killed. It was his birthday too. How fucking shady is that?"

I shook my head slowly. "Damn, Inez. That could've been one of us, you know," I said.

Inez did not respond. She just took a sip of her hot tea and swallowed it slowly. She got out of the bed and went to the bathroom.

My cell phone buzzed on my nightstand. I looked at the caller ID before answering. It was Jayshaun.

"What's up?" I asked.

"Where the fuck you at?" he asked.

"I'm at home," I answered. "And who the hell do you think you are, calling my phone like you my man?"

"Just open the gotdamn door," Jayshaun demanded.

"Open the door? What door?"

"The front door, stupid. I'm outside."

I got out of the bed and went to the front door to see if Jayshaun was really standing there. To my surprise and horror, he was. His friends Romeo and Murder were behind him. I let them in and headed back toward my bedroom.

Jayshaun followed me as his boys made themselves comfortable and sat down on my couch.

"Where the fuck you been?" he asked, grabbing my shoulder and turning me around to face him. "You ain't called a nigga and asked him for some money."

"I've been here, Jay," I replied in irritation. Who did Jayshaun think he was, trying to be the boss in my home?

"You ain't working at Eye Candy no more," Jayshaun said, even though he already knew that. That was ancient news.

"Nah, I ain't," I said, walking out of the room and going into the living room.

"So where do you work? Or should I ask, Who you been getting your money from? Another nigga? You going through his pockets too?" Jayshaun followed me. "And why are you walking away from me?"

I went back into the living room, sat down in an open chair, and ignored Jayshaun. He sat on the second couch near Romeo.

Inez came out of the bathroom and walked into the living room. She looked confused about who was here and turned to me for answers.

"Who the hell is that?" Jayshaun asked me.

"Inez, this is Jayshaun. Jayshaun, this is Inez," I introduced.

"What the fuck is she doing here?" he asked.

"She lives here, fool!" I exclaimed.

"What the hell?" Murder laughed. "You only got one bedroom. Where does she sleep?"

"We share the same bed," I answered.

Jayshaun, Murder, and Romeo laughed. Inez and I exchanged looks of agony. They were so immature, it was disturbing.

"Damn, Jay, I ain't know yo' bitch went both ways," Romeo joked.

"I don't, you li'l buster, so shut the fuck up!" I yelled at him.

"Man, Jayshaun, you betta check dat bitch or else I'm gon' fuck her up and that's on Cedar Block Piru, blood."

"Both of y'all shut up," Jayshaun commanded.

"Cedar Block Piru?" Inez asked. "Y'all niggas shot up the party last night!"

"Hell yeah, did it for the hood. Cedar Block," Murder said, proud of what happened.

"That was some crazy shit, huh?" Jayhsaun shook hands with Murder and Romeo.

Inez and I looked at each other in disgust. Before she could do something that would get her ass beat, I decided to confront Jayshaun, since I knew him better. Inez didn't know, but these fools would slap a female.

I got up to Jayshaun and shoved his face with my hand. "Did you know we were at that party? We coulda been killed!" I screamed.

Jayshaun got up and slammed me up against the wall, holding my wrist in his hands. "What the fuck were you doing at that party anyway, Theori? You my girl, you ain't supposed to be fucking with no bitch-ass crabs!"

I answered, "Me and Inez were invited!"

"You a damn lie!" Jayshaun said, slamming me up against the wall again.

Out the corner of my eye, I saw Inez put her hand over her mouth in fear and Jayshaun's boys just looking as if it was all a game.

Jayshaun continued, "Theori, I know you stripping at parties. The homies from Bompton Mob told me. So why didn't you tell me you had a new job?"

"You knew we was dancing at the Palmer Blocc party?" I sobbed.

"Nah," Jayshaun said. "We wouldn't have shot it up if I knew. And if I did know I woulda dragged you and ya homegirl out of there butt naked."

"Don't bring me into this," Inez said. "You ain't my boyfriend."

"He ain't mine neither," I said, trying to break

free of the grasp he had on me "And you need to let me go, Jay."

"Or else what?" Jayshaun asked.

I was silent.

He continued, "Exactly. Theori, you know I got mad love for you. You my girl. I had your back way back then, and I got your back now, and I'm gon' have your back in the future. I just don't like you doing stupid shit like this that could get you killed."

"How do you know what's gonna kill me and what's not?" I yelled.

"You seen what happened last night. You think we meant to kill ol' boy? We was tryin'a murk somebody else. Bullets don't have names," Jayshaun said, admitting his mistake. "I don't want you getting in the way or getting into some stupid shit."

"So what is that supposed to mean?" I asked, looking at the floor.

"I want you to stop stripping," Jayshaun answered.

I shook my head. "No, I won't."

Jayshaun let me loose. He looked at his boys, looked at me again, and shook his head. "That's wassup, then. C'mon, blood. Let's go," he said to Romeo and Murder.

They followed Jayshaun out the door.

Inez ran over to me and asked me if I was okay. I told her I was fine, but I would feel a lot better if we laid off the stripping and parties for the next couple of weeks.

Crooked Ways

Now rejuvenated and revitalized, Inez and I were back at it again. We were working parties every other weekend.

We were back on top, being Compton's sexiest duo. Word had been spreading around swiftly. We had females trying to be on our team, but we refused to turn this into an agency. It was Theori and Inez only. Besides, the less people working, the more money. That's what it's all about, the money.

Ask me how Crook's old ass found out about us, and I wouldn't even be able to tell you. I ran into him at the Compton Swap Meet when I was buying some lingerie pieces for me and Inez.

"Hey, Redbone, how have you been doing?" Crook asked, catching me coming out of the lingerie shop.

"Um, if you didn't know, it's Theori, and I'm doing fabulous," I said. "How are you?"

Crook answered, "Good, really good." He looked at his two bodyguards, or should I say bitches, and said, "Y'all say hi to *Theori*."

"Don't be a smart-ass," I said, rolling my eyes. "What the hell do you want?"

"I heard you and Mickey been dancing at private parties nowadays," Crook said.

"It ain't Mickey no more. Her name is Inez, and where did you hear that?" I asked, knowing there were numerous options, because so many people were speaking up on our little business.

"You know don't nothing get past Crook in the streets of Compton." He smirked.

Oh please! Your old OG-outdated ass? I thought. *And what the hell you doing rocking that 1970s pimp suit like you Superfly? Time done past you by, brotha!*

"Is that right?"

"Yeah, so how is that going for y'all?"

"Better than ever. Things are, in fact, going spectacular. I'm my own boss! Get a load of that shit! You know muthafuckas really pay to see us . . . anywhere we go," I bragged.

Crook nodded his head. "Would you like to come back to Eye Candy? Just to see if you can get back into the swing of things?

"Hell nah. I like the way I'm swinging nowadays," I replied.

"I'm sure you and Inez aren't making as much money as you were at my strip club," Crook said, so sure of himself.

"Oh believe it, honey! We're making more, Crook. We wouldn't come back to Eye Candy if you paid us. Sorry, Crook, no fuckin' way," I said, walking away.

He grabbed my arm. "C'mon, Red—I mean, Theori. You sure?"

"Hell, yeah."

"Just try it out again."

"Crook, don't beg. That's just low."

"All right, bitch. I had enough of your stank-ass attitude. I'm asking you one more time," Crook said, tightening the grip on my arm.

"And I'm asking you once," I said, gritting my teeth. "You betta let me go before I get one of my niggas to kill your old ass."

Crook let me loose. "Fine, have it your way," he said with a grin.

"Oh, I will," I said. "And you better not try no stupid shit, or else I'll get your ass myself."

Crook watched me sashay off.

Take that for some payback, beeyotch! I thought.

Mister Marcus

It had been about a month since I ran into Crook at the swap meet. I had heard numerous rumors about Eye Candy on its way to closing down. I would be so glad if it did. It would serve his ass right. I also had not seen or heard from Jayshaun, which was odd. I was starting to think he was dead in an alley somewhere, just waiting for his lifeless body to be found. Maybe all of his wild ways had finally caught up to him and ended his life. I never called him after the incident at my house, so maybe he was just being as stubborn as me, waiting for me to punk out and call him first.

I had taken this crisp and sunny day to go shopping on Melrose. I had worked hard for the money, the bills were paid, and I would've been bored out of my mind if I'd stayed home. Inez was up in San Jose visiting her family. I was out all day, just blowing spare cash on the latest fashions from the hottest designers. A little girl from Compton was coming up in the world.

My year at Compton Community College was

almost up. I had been faithfully saving money for
UCLA and working toward bettering my future.

I parked in the apartment parking space I had
claimed since before my parents moved out. I
should've been home much earlier than almost
midnight. The only reason for coming in the house
during the wee hours of the morning was because
of the parties I danced at. Any other time you
would not dare catch me out on the streets of
Compton by myself. I left my shopping bags in the
trunk to risk the agony of being harassed or
jumped for what I had.

I quickly walked toward my apartment and saw
the group of young high school boys blocking my
front door. They were obviously here for my next-
door neighbor, Bone, but they felt it necessary to
hang out on my porch. I excused them and waited
for the back talk to come.

"Damn, li'l mama. My bad," Ray said.

I recognized his face from my senior year at
Compton High when we looked at each other.

"Theori?"

"What's up, Ray?" I responded nonchalantly.

"Chillin', bangin', and slangin', you know," Ray
said, holding the forty to his dark smoker's lips.
"You want some?"

"Nah, I'm good. I do need y'all to back away
from my door. Y'all ain't here to see me," I said,
giving all five of the guys attitude.

"You don't know that," one of them said. "We
could be here to see you."

"But you're not," I said, taking the keys out of
my purse. "I don't fuck with them young heads,
only grown men."

"Theori, what are you talkin' 'bout? I am a grown man," Ray replied.

"Not by still being in high school, and you hanging around these young-ass boys," I replied, rolling my eyes at him.

One of the boys slapped my ass. "Damn, you thick, li'l mama."

"You better not touch me, nigga! I don't know you like that. I only know Ray, and he's not even allowed to touch me like that," I said, raising my voice. "Ray, you and your li'l friends better get up out of here. You know this area got Piru written all over it, and remember, you don't fuck with Bloods."

"Bitch, who the fuck you talking to?" another boy yelled. "Damn right, you don't know us like that. Don't be telling us where to be. I will—"

"You ain't gon' do shit, but get the hell up out of my area, you ol' punk-ass crab!" I yelled.

I immediately felt like I had signed my death certificate. They all started hollering and cursing.

I couldn't get my key in the door fast enough. Someone grabbed me, flung me around, and pinned me to my door. I almost cried when I saw Ray grab his pistol, tucked into the basketball shorts underneath his jeans.

Suddenly, another man, whose face I was sure I had seen before parted through and backed them away from me. "Ay, what the hell is y'all doing, man? This is my girl, Theori."

Ray was surprised. "Ah, for real? I was just about to pistol-whip the bitch for calling us crabs. She was out of line for that bullshit."

"Shut the fuck up, man," my savior shouted. "Y'all bitch-ass niggas is out of line for bringing

y'all asses to this area. Get the fuck out of here before East Side Piru have to kill y'all asses. Y'all
dem same mark-ass niggas that come over here
spray painting y'all hood on our walls and shit. Ya
boy Bone gon' get fucked up now that I know he
ain't a Piru nigga, perpetratin' and shit. Get the
fuck out of here!"

They had nothing to say after his rampage and
threats. They mumbled and went on their way,
leaving the apartment complex. My hero watched
them leave and looked at his boys standing by the
apartment standing two doors down.

"You alright, Theori?" he asked.

"Yeah, thank you," I said. "Let me ask you. How
do you know my name?"

He chuckled. "Don't nothing get past Killa Mark
in the streets of Compton."

I smiled uncomfortably and tried my best to remember where I had heard those words before.
"What's your name?"

"They call me Killa Mark," he said, looking me
up and down.

"No, not your hood name." I giggled falsely. "I
meant your real name."

"Marcus."

"Hold up," I said as a memory came to mind. I
grabbed hold of his right arm and beheld the tattoo I recognized almost a year and some change
ago when I was working at Eye Candy. "Killa
Mark, did you use to go to the Eye Candy?"

"I went a few times way back when," he answered. I could hear the uneasiness in his voice.

"You remember a stripper named Redbone?" I
asked, hoping his answer would be yes.

"Nah, not really," he said, looking at his boys.

"Oh, well then," I said, embarrassed. "Never mind. Thanks again. I'm gonna go inside now." I rolled my eyes in humiliation as I turned around to pick my keys up off of the ground.

"Well, hold up, cutie," Marcus said. "We chillin' at my boy's house right now. You wanna come over?"

I was hesitant, but I figured everything would be alright. My apartment was only two doors down, so if anybody pulled any funny business I could just run there. "Sure, why not?" I shrugged my shoulders and followed him down the hall.

He greeted his friends. "What's good, blood?"

"Shit, nuttin," his homeboy snorted.

"Theori, this is Cadillac, Byron, and the homie Li'l Crook. This right here, y'all, is Theori," Marcus introduced.

I gave a slight wave and took the nods of their heads as a "Hello."

We entered the apartment, which I later found out belonged to Byron. I sat next to Marcus on the couch, Cadillac sat in a chair at the kitchen table, Byron shuffled some cards at the poker table, and Li'l Crook stood in the entrance of the hallway.

"Where did you go to school?" Cadillac asked. "You look real familiar."

"Compton High."

"Nah, that's where I went, blood," Byron said. "I ain't never seen yo' ass there."

"That's 'cuz yo' ass never went to school," Marcus laughed.

"True," Byron said after shrugging his shoulders.

"Oh," Cadillac said, carrying on his conversation with me, "I went to Centennial."

"Then you might've heard of my girl Inez, Inez Barrera?" I asked.

Cadillac thought for a little bit and then said, "Light-skinned mixed bitch? Yeah, everyone knows Inez."

"Why'd you say it like that?"

"Is that your best friend?"

"Maybe."

"Then I ain't telling you."

"Just say it. You might as well," I said.

"Fine then," Cadillac agreed. "Inez ain't nothing but a gold digging ho."

"And proud of it," I defended. I, too, was a gold digging ho. I didn't care what anybody had to say.

"Shut up, Lac. Don't be saying that shit," Marcus said.

"Remember she was in that video shoot for Dayton? She had like a little cameo or something," Byron said, remembering seeing Inez in LA rapper Dayton's video. "She looked like a straight ghetto girl. Hood rat!"

I couldn't believe these no-good niggas were disrespecting my best friend right in front of my face.

"Fuck Inez! The baddest bitch in that video was Kirrah. Y'all remember her?" Marcus asked.

"Yeah, that chlamydia chick," Cadillac joked. "Bet she ain't shooting no videos no more. She mighta burned Dayton. Word on the street was, he got that chlamydia shit."

"Or maybe he burned her. That's probably how she got it," I said, adding to the conversation.

"Inez look better than Kirrah, though," Li'l Crook said. "Anybody can see that."

"She lives with me too," I said, just deciding to put it out there.

Trying to change the subject, Marcus said, "So what do you do for a living, Theori?"

"I dance. Both me and Inez dance at private parties," I answered. I was surprised they hadn't heard of us. I thought damn near everyone knew. Plus, he'd known my name and said nothing got past him in the hood.

"For real? What kind of parties? Bachelor parties?" Byron asked.

"Any kind of party, preferably the kind of parties when niggas from the hood wanna get with their homies and have some entertainment," I responded.

I hung out around the house a little more and got to know Marcus and his boys a little better. I was attracted to his rough and dangerous look. Hopefully, he was feeling me too and we could take it to another level.

The time was approaching three in the morning. I yawned and wondered why the hell all of the guys were not as tired as I was. Marcus looked at me and saw the need for sleep in my eyes. He offered to walk me to my apartment, and I gladly accepted. I said good-bye to Cadillac, Byron, and Li'l Crook. Marcus and I walked out the door and toward my apartment.

"Aw, thanks for walking me two doors down," I said sarcastically.

"Well, ain't you sleepy? I wanted to make sure

you didn't pass out on your way here." Marcus laughed.

"Right, whatever." I stood in the doorway and faced him after I opened the door. "Marcus, what if I told you I wanted to fuck you right now? What would you say?"

"I'd say you are a really honest person," he answered.

I went into the house and put my hand on the second wooden door. "Nice, but that's not the answer I wanted to hear," I said, closing the door.

Marcus stopped the door with his foot and said, "And I would also say that I wanna fuck you too."

With that made clear, I pulled Marcus into the apartment and slammed the front door shut. My body was yearning for his manhood. After all, it had been a year and a half since I had last had sex. I had been abstinent from sex for a solid time now, and I was ready.

"It's been awhile since I had sex, you know," I moaned as he kissed my neck.

"I find that hard to believe," Marcus said in between kisses.

I wondered to myself if he was trying to call me loose, or just say I was that damn tempting and sexy that it was hard to believe. "You'll feel what I mean when you put it in," I said.

"Let the pussy talk for itself," Marcus said.

He didn't waste any time after saying that. He found my bedroom, leading *me* there, imagine that, and took me down.

After I had experienced the thing I hadn't felt in so long, I went straight to sleep in his arms.

* * *

We woke up side by side the next morning.

"Man, you really ain't had sex in a minute," Marcus said when we did a recap of last night. "That shit was so good and tight; it was like fucking a virgin."

I smiled. "I told you."

"Yeah, you were real nice and tight," he said with a yawn.

"Yup, you wasn't too bad yourself."

"Get outta here with that. Killa Mark got skills," he bragged. "Check this out, though. I'ma throw a li'l party . . . I wanna see you and ol' girl there."

"All right, as long as you got some cash. When is it gonna be, Marcus?" I asked. I made sure to let him know from the get-go, no cash, no flash.

"I'm gon' have it at Cadillac's crib on Saunders Street and Bradfield Avenue by Leuders Park," Marcus answered. "We be chillin' over his house all the time. It'll be the same ol'-same ol', only with some live entertainment instead of a porno."

"And more people, right?" I asked.

"If you count you and your girl. It's only gon' be me, Lac, Byron, Li'l Crook, Eric, and Monte," Marcus replied.

"No girls?" I asked.

"You and Inez! I know you ain't scared. These is the niggas that got some real money to put in your pocket." Marcus chuckled.

I smiled nervously. "Hell nah, I ain't scared. Don't act like y'all doing big things, 'cuz if you was, then you wouldn't be living in Compton, claiming Leuders Park Piru," I said.

"Keep on disrespecting the hood like that. You gon' mess around, get fucked up by one of these niggas, like you almost did last night," Marcus warned.

I rolled my eyes. "So when is this party, oops, get-together gonna be?"

"Next Friday night," Marcus answered.

"Oh, cool," I replied. "Inez should be back out here by that time."

"That's wassup then," Marcus said. He slapped me on my ass. "Now get up and cook a nigga some breakfast."

Sleeping with the

Enemy

Thursday night approached and there was no sign of Inez. She didn't call me to let me know when she was coming home. I would've thought she'd be back from San Jose by now. I gave her a call to find out when she was coming home.

"What's up, Theori?"

"Inez, when you coming back?"

"Girl, I'ma leave Saturday morning," Inez answered. "Why? Wassup?"

"Inez, this sexy-ass nigga from Leuders Park wants us to come dance tomorrow night. He ain't having no major party, just a few niggas from his hood," I answered.

"Ah, nah, girl, I'm still gonna be in San Jose. I got to stay for my aunt's big fortieth birthday party. You should've told me sooner, babe."

"Yeah, I know; that was my fault. I should've told you when he first mentioned it."

Inez said, "Well, shit, Theori. Go ahead and handle that then. It's only a couple of them. You can work that, can't you?"

"Yeah," I answered. "No! We never worked parties alone before, and I ain't gonna start."

"We can use the money. Think about it, it's just money in our pocket. Do it, Theori. Don't you know the guy who wants you to come?" Inez asked.

"Yeah, I slept with him." I laughed. "Fuck it, I'll do it then. I won't stay long."

"That's what I'm talkin' 'bout, mami! Get that money!" Inez screeched. "Call me tomorrow morning."

"All right, bye."

I got off the phone with Inez and went on to sleep. The next afternoon, I woke up and spent the rest of the afternoon getting ready for the Leuders Park Piru get-together. Underneath my jeans and my hoodie, I wore a black tanga panty and a lacy push-up bra.

I was scared about being the only girl at this event. I had never stripped alone, with the exception of Eye Candy. I did feel relieved that Marcus would be there, and with the fact that we'd slept together, I could have a sense of security.

I was in a rush. I thought I would have time, but I got caught up. I hurried up and put on my heels. As I was walking out of the door, Marcus called my cell phone.

"Hey, Marcus," I answered.

"Where da fuck you at, man?" he yelled over the television.

"I'm running late, I'm sorry," I said, rushing to my car.

"You lost or something?" he asked.

"Nah, I actually haven't even left yet," I answered. "I'm just now getting in my car."

"Hurry up," Marcus said. He then hung up.

I sighed and put my phone in my purse. I got in the car and sped over to the location of the party, the north side of Compton. I got out of the car and walked up to the front door. I rang the doorbell. Cadillac answered the door. He didn't greet me at all. He just let me in and sat down. I observed who was there.

There was a dark-skinned brotha over by the flat screen hanging up on the wall. There was a caramel-complexioned young man sitting on the couch smoking a blunt. Next to him was Byron. Li'l Crook and Marcus were pouring drinks in the kitchen.

Marcus walked over to me. "Damn, Theori, 'bout time you got here," he slurred.

I looked at him and smiled. "Sorry I'm late. You gon' introduce me to your people or what?" I asked seductively.

"Yeah, you know Lac, Byron, and Li'l Crook. On the couch is Monte, and standing up by the TV is Eric," Marcus said.

"Hey, y'all," I said waving.

"So whatchu waiting for?" Marcus pushed me toward the center of the room. "Get this shit started."

The music was already playing. All I had to do was get out of my clothes and strip for these guys. In thirty minutes, I'd jet. That was the plan.

I stripped out of my clothes. I danced, entertained, and took cash in my view. I made their dicks get rock hard. I looked at Marcus, standing in the corner of the room. He was nodding his head to the music, just watching me.

I continued to work the room. The guys started to get too touchy-feely. One of them even proceeded to stick his finger up my vagina. The others followed and did more than just put their finger in it.

"Ay, y'all, don't do that," I said.

"Bitch, please!" Monte said.

I moved their hands. I got up out of my split and walked over to Marcus.

"They can't touch me, Marcus," I told him. "At least not like that."

Marcus rolled his eyes. "All right, y'all, alright, y'all. You can't touch the bitch like that," he said.

"Why she tripping?" Eric asked.

"Nigga, just don't touch the bitch," Marcus said once again.

"Fuck that, nigga," Monte said. "I'm 'bout to go to my girl Quisha house and get me some." He grabbed a bottle of gin and left the house.

Eric followed after and said, "Yeah, blood. I can go to Eye Candy for a show. I'm gone, nigga. This shit was good till the bitch started tripping."

I waited till he shut the front door to speak. "Yo, Marcus, I didn't mean to crash this, but I just ain't feel right letting them feel on my pussy and shit."

Marcus shook his head. "Don't trip, they just some drunk, horny-ass niggas anyway."

"I guess I'm gonna leave too, then," I said, gathering the money to put it away.

"Nah, Theori, stay and drink a little bit with us,"

Li'l Crook requested. "And leave that little outfit on."

I giggled.

By twelve midnight, I was on drink number three. By one in the morning, I was tipsy. I could really hold some liquor.

Marcus lured me into the bedroom down the hall. I figured he wanted some more pussy, and I was ready as hell to give it to him. He tossed me on the bed and got on top of me. He was so forceful, it was scary.

"Marcus, wh-what you doing?" I stuttered.

He pulled down my tanga and put a condom on his hard dick. Before I could push him off, he was already ramming his dick into me. It was hard, rough, and too fast. I told him to slow down, and he only went faster. It became painful, and I begged him to stop.

With a hand pulling my hair and the other pinching my waist, Marcus kept on going. Faster. Faster. Rougher. Once he came, he called Cadillac in.

"She's all yours, blood." He chuckled and tossed him a condom.

I was so weak, I could barely move. I watched Marcus leave as Cadillac put on the condom. Cadillac turned me over and fucked me from behind, calling me all kinds of degrading names as he did. I screamed and hollered and things only intensified him.

When he was done violating me, he yelled for Li'l Crook. Li'l Crook too came in and took advantage of me.

After he got off, he punched me in the face and

said, "That's for my Uncle Crook, bitch! Ay yo, Byron, you wanna hit this bitch?"

Byron entered and raped me brutally. He put bruises all over my body and called for Marcus. Marcus re-entered the room, gave me a couple of blows to the head and a couple of kicks to my stomach. With the help of his boys, he duct-taped my mouth and tied my wrists and ankles. They carried me to a truck, tossed me in the very back, and drove to Leuders Park. They dragged me out of the van and over to the dirty, disgusting and piss-smelling restrooms.

"Cover her eyes with this," Byron said, handing Marcus a red bandana.

"Nah, use the blue one I got so it could look like some crips did it," Li'l Crook said.

Marcus took the blue bandana and tied it around my eyes. "We shoulda covered her eyes before we bought her to the damn park," he said angrily. "And where the fuck is Inez? That bitch said she would be here."

"I am here, nigga," Inez said.

I gasped when I recognized her voice. Someone kicked me in my side. I began to cry.

"Damn," Inez said. "Y'all really fucked her up."

"Bitch, shut up. Here, take this damn gun and break this bitch off," Li'l Crook said, handing Inez a gun. "And Crook said he got your money."

"Inez!" I mumbled.

Inez hit me in the head with the barrel of the gun. "I'm just looking out for me! Crook said he was breaking me off with a lot of cash if I was in on this shit. It was way more cash than what we we're making! This kinda money is worth more than our little friendship. Fuck that and fuck you!"

"Noooo," I moaned. The tears I cried were soaking up the bandana. I wailed like a baby in the last moments of my life.

"Yeah, Theori. You see, that's what it's always been about. The money! I just want the paper," Inez said as she held the gun over my body. "Take this to the bank!"

POP . . . POP!

Someday Soon

"No, Jamal. I don't wanna do it in this nasty restroom! Why couldn't we just stay at my grandma's house?" a young girl said.

"C'mon, girl! It's three in the morning. Ain't nobody gon' see us," he persuaded. "You ain't never tryin'a do nothing with me at all. That's why you couldn't be my girl because you ain't down for shit."

"Why are you acting stupid, Jamal?" she asked as she turned around and slapped her hand against his chest.

"Well, if you loved me you'd do it."

"I don't do that, boy!"

"Whatever. Just try it, Nadinna!"

"Jamal, nooo—" Nadinna screamed when seeing my bloody body soaking in its own blood. She covered her mouth and tried her best not to puke from the bloody sight.

"Oh shit!" Jamal gasped.

"What do we do? Should we call the police?"

Nadinna asked, getting ready to take out her cell phone. "I'm going to call the police."

"Nah, let's just go! I think she's dead already," Jamal said. "That's somebody else's problem. Not ours. You know it's not good to meddle."

"You call this meddling? Jamal, this woman could be dying and you ain't tryin'a do nothing about it? That's foul, man!"

"Let's go, Nadinna. Get the fuck up outta here!"

"Nooo," I moaned with my last ounce of strength. I muffled through the duct tape over my mouth, "Help, please."

"Oh shit, she's still alive, Jamal!" Nadinna said. "I'm calling the cops."

"I'm gone then!" Jamal said, running off.

"Fuck you," Nadinna said as she called the police.

"Thank you," I whispered after she got off the phone with the police and ripped the duct tape off of my mouth.

"You're welcome. Just hang in there," she said. She informed the police station about what she just discovered and informed them of our location. She got off the phone and said, "The police and an ambulance are on the way."

My soul rejoiced at the mercy and grace of God for sparing my life. I vowed that from that day forward, gold digging and stripping all over Compton would not make up who I was or shape who I could be. I had a second chance to do things right. I would give up everything and everyone negative and put the focus on myself and school. That was where my heart really belonged, in school and education. I started off my journey with a goal, which was to get money for school, and somehow my goal shifted course. I planned to get back on the right track so I could do something valuable with my life. Coming close to death scared me back to life, literally.

I would even move to North Carolina with my parents if I had to—well, nah, I love the West Coast—but I could relocate to a better part of the city. Things would be okay, once I put my life back in order. Thank God for second chances, and I knew this was my second wind to do this all over again.

As for Inez, Marcus, Li'l Crook, and the others who had it in for me, I made a vow to myself to put them behind bars for what they did. And the ultimate vengeance was the Lord's. I put it in God's hands and considered it the past. I had to continue to move on with my future.

PART FOUR:

$ $ Life Savers $ $

Volunteer

Kentia looked at her girl Peedi getting ready for the night. Peedi had slid into a halter dress that was cutting right below her behind. Her bronze stilettos were adorned in jewels and crystals. Kentia guessed her outfit was worth more than what she would make tonight prostituting herself. Of the money she made, seventy-five percent of it would go to The Boss.

Peedi could feel Kentia's eyes glaring at her. "What is it, girl?" she asked.

Kentia shook her head. "Oh, nothing really." She turned away and looked around at what had been her new home for a solid month. It seemed like one moment she was high-rolling with big ballers of LA, and the next she was broke and living in a whorehouse, trying to sell dope to fiends and wannabes. Instead of progressing uphill, she was stumbling back down. Just knowing it all could have been avoided with a single move ate her up inside. If she had never left the apartment after

Omar hit her, she'd be on top doing something to earn her more riches.

Working for The Boss had allowed her to get some new clothes, but it didn't compare to what she used to have. She went from shopping in The Hills to not even being able to go to the mall. She never pictured herself being this kind of young woman.

"Look, I know you don't like it here, but where else can you go?" Peedi asked, throwing the truth in her face.

That's what hurt the most. Kentia felt so ashamed and lost that she had stopped talking to her family and few friends out of embarrassment. If the girls she went to high school with found out she went from top-notch to somebody's drug whore, they'd be ready to clown. Shanti offered to let her stay at her place, but Kentia had too much pride, bruised pride. She wanted to show she could be resilient and bounce back from what she named a temporary downfall.

Every day she was reminded of where she came from, to where she was going, to where she was now. After all, she was the only chick who owned a Lexus while they pushed fifteen- to twenty-year-old Saturns and Hondas. She felt out of place, and knew she was, but this was her home.

"You're right," Kentia agreed. "Where you stationed at tonight?" She tried to give her the impression that she took her job almost as serious as she did.

"San Pedro and Main Street."

"That Mexican area?" she joked.

"Hey, whoever pays."

"Word? Make that money, girl."

"Oh, I got to!"

"Are you by yourself?"

"No, Diamond is coming with me, and Dave is going to be watching us in a car around the corner," Peedi answered. "Why? Were you thinking about getting into this line of duty?"

"Hell no. I'm fine with selling drugs," Kentia said truthfully. "But if I would've known The Boss had women in the house selling clothes, I would have done that shit instead. He just put me down with drugs, you know?"

"Well, now you balanced out the house. Three women selling clothes, three women selling drugs, and three women selling sex."

Kentia frowned up her face at Peedi. She spoke of it so lightly, as if it were moral and a lot of females did it. But that was the problem. There were innumerable females who had made the not-so-respectable decision to do this. Kentia was one of hundreds in Los Angeles alone.

In came one of the prettiest girls in the house, Stephanie. She was Panamanian and Black with a nice short haircut, ebony eyes, and almond-colored skin. She was holding her face in her hands, crying like a baby.

"What's wrong, sweetie?" Kentia asked, running to her side.

"The Boss is kicking me out!" she wailed as she began packing her one bag. "This isn't right! It's not fair!"

"What? Why?" Kentia asked. She was hurt that Stephanie was crying, but devastated that she had to leave because she had grown the closest to her.

"He asked me to make a move over in Compton, but I refused because it's my little boy's birthday and I promised my mother I'd be there to celebrate it," she said.

Kentia could barely see those ebony eyes that sparkled when Stephanie smiled. Her eyes were closed tight and tears still managed to fall to her chin.

"Do you have a place to go?" Kentia put her arm around her.

"My mom said I could never come back, only to see my son, after she kicked me out six months ago. And I can't go back to my baby's father. I just can't."

"Why not, Steph?"

She only shook her head. "I just can't." Images of her baby's father abusing her unmercifully and forcing her to snort coke popped into her head. She wiped her eyes and took a long, sorrowful sigh.

Kentia wanted to do something because she felt for this girl. Stephanie was at her last draw, but Kentia felt she had a good hand. So she excused herself and went to see The Boss.

She knocked twice before he allowed her to enter.

He told her to sit in the chair across from his cherry wood desk. "Kentia."

"Hey, I heard you need a runner for some deal in Compton."

"Maybe."

"I can do it."

"You want to?"

"Only if you let Stephanie stay."

"You tryin'a make a deal with me?'

"More like a trade-off."

"Are you the boss?"

"No, sir."

"So where in the fuck do you get the idea that you can come up in here and negotiate with me?"

"But it works out. You get to keep a worker and have someone making that move."

"Still negotiating. And I got bitches lined up around the corner that can easily replace you and Stephanie."

"I apologize, Boss."

He sighed and then there was an awkward moment of silence.

"I admire your loyalty to your co-workers. That's why I'm going to let you make the trip to Compton."

"Does Steph get to keep her job? And go to her son's birthday party?"

"She can go to her son's party while you're out making the run. Now if you fuck this up, Steph loses her job, and so do you. Both of y'all will be getting kicked out ASAP if something goes wrong. I got a lot of compassion for my ladies, but if I were you, I wouldn't be so quick to take another's place."

Kentia took those words to heart and believed him to the fullest. He told her to get ready and get the drugs from his guard, Derek. She went into the room and told Stephanie to stop crying and stop packing up the little bit of her belongings.

"You can stay and you still have your job. Now get ready for your son's party," Kentia said.

"What?" asked a startled Stephanie.

"I took that job," Kentia said, laughing to herself because she too sounded like this was a legit career.

"Kentia, no!" she gasped.

"What? Why not?"

"Why the hell did you do that?"

"Because, I didn't want you to leave and neither did you!"

"Kentia, this is more than delivering drugs to some man in Compton. Girl, this could be life or death!" Stephanie's Panamanian accent was more present than ever.

Kentia could tell she was more disappointed than happy. Kentia shook her head. "What are you talking about?"

Stephanie informed her that Compton, being the hot and always-armed city that it was, was no place for female drug dealers to be. The last worker sent to Compton by The Boss was murdered after two men robbed her of the drugs. This alone put strong fear in Kentia.

"I'm not saying it could happen to you, but it's too dangerous. Damn, Kentia."

"Boss said if I fuck up then I'm out of here," Kentia informed. "So you best believe for damn sure I'm gonna be on point and on guard." She decided not to say that The Boss included her in the deal because she truly planned on carrying out this order.

"Please be careful, girl. Out of all these bitches in here, you the only one I care about," Stephanie said.

Kentia embraced her because her feelings were mutual. "Girl, me too. Only you and Peedi. Everything is cool, I promise." They both took sighs of relief. "Now, how old is your son turning?"

"Three," Stephanie answered.

"Tell him I said happy birthday."

"I will."

"I better go see Derek," Kentia said as she dressed up in some sweats and a tank top. She borrowed a pair of Stephanie's Jordans and slipped them on. She looked in the mirror. There wasn't a feeling of confidence when she looked in the mirror. Now that she was living in the house, she felt insecure. She tried to feel good, but couldn't. Instead of looking flyy, she aimed at looking plain. She didn't want to stand out, now that she was a drug dealer. She had to look like the average young female dressed on a cool night.

She gave Stephanie one last hug and left the room. She went into the kitchen where she saw Derek bagging up who knows how many pounds of coke, black tar heroin, and ecstasy pills. He put the bags of drugs into empty food boxes of Cheese Nips and Premium crackers and placed the bags of ecstasy tablets into prescription medicine boxes. He then dumped the fake groceries into two grocery bags, paper inside plastic.

"This is for real. Some major shit, Kentia. You gotta take the bus like a normal person. Pretend like you actually came from the grocery store. Set the bags under your legs, or next to your feet," Derek said.

"Which bus do I catch?" I asked.

"Catch the western bus all the way down to Imperial. Catch that bus down to Atlantic Avenue. From Atlantic Avenue you're gonna get on the bus headed south toward Compton and go down to Rosecrans. Get off on Rosecrans and walk to Long Beach Boulevard. They live at this address." He handed Kentia a sheet of paper with thorough bus routes and the address to Marcus' house. "His name is Marcus and he's from Leuders Park Piru. Ring the doorbell once and knock three times so he won't come out shooting."

Kentia's eyes lit up. "Are you serious?"

Derek joked, "Nah, I was only kidding. But all seriousness, this move is no laughing matter. Do what you got to do and get the hell out of there. The Boss doesn't really like sending his women to Compton under these conditions."

"Why can't I just drive there?"

Derek shrugged. "The Boss ain't going to let you drive his car!"

"His car? Last I recall, he ain't paid for shit on my ride," Kentia protested.

"Yeah, when he let you live in this house that shit became his. Don't make me have to get your contract. Do your thang and get back. By the time everything is said and done, you should be back by nine-thirty. Just try to get back before ten because buses start running hella slow, and I don't want you waiting in Compton till midnight."

Kentia left the house at eight on the dot. She got on the bus and hoped to be in Compton's soon.

Bettering Lives

With Simone by her side, Kirrah started the organization *Affected*, designed for women emotionally and or physically affected by men, STDs, or any other burden. It was a support group created with women in mind. Women who had been through something and survived it could now unite with women who were in their own personal struggle or young girls who had yet to go through. Affected and its spokeswomen held seminars throughout Southern California at local high schools, community colleges, and some universities.

Instead of trying out for the BET competition, Kirrah felt she could start her career off doing something of her own where she could help those closest in proximity to her. Benny helped fund the organization and had already began getting them public attention.

This Friday, Kirrah and Simone along with two other ladies, had visited the city of Compton. They had just held a seminar at Centennial High School, where girls poured their hearts and eyes out as they opened up about life, insecurity, drugs, sexuality, men, family, abuse, and other lingering pains. By the end of the session, over half of the girls had found peace with themselves and each other.

By four in the afternoon, they had set up at Compton Community College, where they would hold another seminar for the slightly older crowd. Musical performances were arranged from students at the El Camino music program on the Compton campus. What better way to show success in these mean streets than through local talent?

Eight o'clock had just hit and the session was on its way to a close. A Hispanic woman with an undeniably gorgeous face and flattering figure was opening up about her personal experience. At age fifteen, she had made the worst decision to join a gang. She relived how devastated her father was when word reached his ears. She admitted to sleeping with the male gang members just to gain acceptance, since her father began to disown her. By the end of her story she had the whole room teary-eyed.

She left on this last note: "I've established a new relationship with my father and I love him so much. I know what I've done in the past, and I don't look back. I move forward. There's a man who's loved me unconditionally, even when my biological father had shut me out. He's loved me through it all, *Jesús Cristo*, and he's the only man I've ever loved back." She took a tissue and wiped her eyes.

The crowd applauded as she sat down to approving smiles and friendly pats on the back.

Kirrah stood up and closed out the session. "Before we depart, I want you to know that everything that happened in your past needs to be released. Some of us walk around with a load on our shoulders, and we're stuck in that moment. We have to let go and move on. Cry it out, write it out, hell, shout it out! But in order to achieve success in the future, we need to let go of the failures in our past."

There was one woman who felt as if Kirrah was talking directly to her. She had heard of the ex-video model and had seen her in videos, but had never seen her in person. She sat wide-eyed and attentive and even took notes. She scribbled Kirrah's last statement at the end of her notes. That would be her new life statement. She took it upon herself to speak with Kirrah as the other guests socialized amongst each other.

"Thank you so much," she said, taking Kirrah by surprise and grabbing her in a hug. "Really, thank you."

"You're so welcome," Kirrah answered. "What's your name?"

"Theori Cameron," she answered.

"You have amazing eyes. Do you go to school here?" Kirrah asked, taking a water bottle from off the stage. She opened it up and took a small sip.

"For now, but I'm going back to UCLA next year," Theori answered. "But I'm so grateful for you guys being here. I feel so much better knowing that I'm not in this boat alone."

Kirrah replied, "Well, there's nothing new under the sun, as quoted in the Holy Word. I just wanted the chance to help someone."

Theori began, "Yes, I wanted to share my story, but I was too ashamed."

"Stop right there! Don't ever be ashamed. Be encouraged and driven by what you went through because, if it wasn't for that, you wouldn't be where you are today," corrected Kirrah.

"Well, I was shy and scared. Kirrah, you just don't know how hurt I've been. I've had a best friend stab me in the back. No, shot me, literally, and left me for dead." Theori pulled down the strap of her shirt to expose the bullet wounds in her shoulder and arm.

"It's a miracle you're even alive," Kirrah said. She took Theori's hand and led her to the stairs of the stage. They sat down. "Tell me everything."

"No, I couldn't."

"And why the hell not? Why should you keep this on your heart while the person who did it to you walks around free to live their lives a happy individual?"

"I haven't opened up before."

"Well, now is the time to speak up and be heard."

It took a little more convincing, but eventually Theori told Kirrah everything, from her parents leaving California to lying up in the hospital bed after being shot. Kirrah was in awe of her story.

"Girl, I'm working my case up with my lawyer, and I'm gonna put those muthafuckas in jail! But police, supposedly, can't find them and they suspect they are hiding. They questioned Crook, and he claims he was in Vegas at the time. Ain't that about nothing?" Theori laughed with relief, finally being able to open up her heart.

"And after all that, you've managed to take control of your life and get your education?"

Theori nodded humbly. "That's been my goal all along, but it was promoted by the wrong motivation. I only wanted the cash to fix myself up and pay for my education and apartment. I shouldn't have gone about it that way. I let myself slip. I got further and further away from school to the point where I forgot all about it. I was a gold digger. I don't ever wanna be that way again."

Kirrah was touched and agreed. "Oh, I feel the exact same way. I wouldn't go back to that lifestyle if they paid me. All it left me with was bad rep, tears, and an STD."

"But you can make up for all that now. Don't you feel satisfied?" Theori asked.

"More than ever. Are you working, Theori?" Kirrah asked.

"Yes, I work at an elementary school as a substitute teacher."

"I'm glad you got a job, especially working with children."

"Well, let me tell you," Theori joked. "Not every child in Compton is a saint."

Kirrah laughed. "I believe it. I'm from Inglewood, and at my elementary school I was a handful and full of it. And in high school, I was a hot mess. I was an arrogant little bitch, no lie! It only worsened once I started shooting music videos. Ooh, girl, you couldn't tell me nothing."

Theori smiled. "Seriously?"

"Yes, but enough about me. I wanna ask you something. In your spare time, would you be willing to join Affected and engage in our seminars and sessions?"

Theori felt warm inside and grinned. "I'd like that very much. Shit, when can I start?"

They laughed.

Kirrah answered, "Next week we're going to Santa Monica High and then the college."

"I'm all in."

"Great."

They exchanged numbers, and Theori offered her dinner at her apartment.

"Now I do live in the hood, but it is home," Theori forewarned. "I am moving to Carson in a month."

"Girl, I ain't tripping." Kirrah laughed. "But I hope you don't mind waiting about thirty minutes to an hour because I have to clean up around here."

"That's fine, and it gives me just enough time to prepare and cook dinner," Theori answered.

"Cool, I'll call you for directions when I'm done. Put your number in my phone."

Theori did as told and said goodbye. "All right, see you later."

Brewing Trouble

Kentia said a silent prayer as she paced the streets of Compton nervously. She felt as if every car passing by and every person that laid eyes on her knew she was carrying drugs in her grocery bags. She wished she had never volunteered to do this for The Boss.

She quickly walked down Rosecrans Avenue toward Long Beach Boulevard, hoping to reach Marcus' home soon. Dogs barked, thugs whistled, and cars honked. Kentia kept walking and even quickened her pace. She reached the complex and went to the front door of her destination. She rang once and knocked three times. It took a moment, but someone opened the door.

"Who the fuck are you?"

"Kentia. The Boss sent me," she answered. "Is Marcus here?"

"You talking to him. That's my shit in your bags?" he asked, opening the door so she could enter.

"Yes, sir," she stated as if she were talking to The Boss himself.

Marcus chuckled. "Come in."

"Nah, I got to hurry back. If I could just have the money, that'll be cool."

"Come in. I ain't gon' say it no more," Marcus said.

Kentia obeyed and followed Marcus into the house. They went into the kitchen. Kentia set the bags on the table and Marcus called for Li'l Crook and Cadillac. He introduced them to Kentia, and then took out the drugs.

"The Boss needs his money," Kentia reminded him.

The men laughed. Marcus said, "Yeah, we know. Don't worry, he'll get his paper."

Kentia smiled, but it was forced. She smelled the foulness in the air, and felt it in the atmosphere. She knew something wasn't right. To hopefully make herself feel less awkward, she made conversation. "So, who is all this for? For you?"

"You heard of a man named Crook?" Li'l Crook asked. "He's my uncle. It's for him."

"He must be getting paid out the ass! What does he do?" Kentia smiled, hoping to ease their cold hearts.

"Owns a failing strip club," Lac answered.

"Shut the fuck up! That shit is back up on bank since Mickey went back."

"Mickey? Who is that?" Kentia asked.

"Why you being so nosey?" Marcus neatly opened up a package of coke.

"I apologize."

"How much do I owe again?" Marcus asked.

Kentia remembered the amount and replied, "Fifty thousand."

Marcus nodded. "All right. Let me go to the bedroom and get your money. Hey, niggas, watch our little friend Kentia and make sure she doesn't go anywhere." He left the kitchen.

Kentia was instructed to make herself comfortable and sit down at the kitchen table. She refused and was then demanded to sit. To avoid conflict, she did as told.

Marcus returned about five minutes later, interrupting the deadening silence.

Kentia turned around and was staring down the barrel of gun. She almost lost her breath and gasped for air.

"The Boss and Crook have some unsettled business, and you just got involved," Marcus said with such force, it was frightening.

"Why I got to get in this shit? Go after The Boss, not me! I didn't do shit to you," Kentia bravely stated. She decided that she was going to live her last moments with a sharp tongue. "Don't be no bitches!"

Marcus, Li'l Crook, and Cadillac laughed.

"This is a brave muthafucka, nigga!" Li'l Crook said as his partners agreed. "Damn, bitch, do you know who you fuckin' with?"

"Some punk asses who work for some guy named Crook who too scared to deal with The Boss, so they go through his worker! What, you 'pose to be a *G* for dat?" Kentia exclaimed.

"Let her talk shit. This shit is amusing. Besides, she living her last minutes anyway," Marcus said.

"I will talk shit then muthafucka!" Kentia yelled.

"So why my boss and your owner, Cook or Cake or whatever, got beef?"

"That Boss nigga grew up down the street from Crook. They wanted to go into business together and open up a strip joint after they graduated high school. They copped a loan from Crook's grandfather in '99. But The Boss flaked out and took over half of the loan and moved out of Compton to LA and started his own shit. He left Crook with damn near nothing. In the hood, that's disrespect, and payback is a bitch!" Li'l Crook reported.

Kentia shrugged her shoulders. "Sounds like a personal problem to me."

"Only reason why Crook didn't kill his ass earlier was 'cuz he was in jail for robbing a bank! Tryin'a start his strip club," Li'l Crook said.

"And I'm supposed to give a flying fuck?"

"Can we bust this ho wide open now?" Lac asked.

"Be easy. Shit, we just came out of hiding from cappin' that bitch, Theori. And word from Crook is, she still living because the police took him in for questioning. When we kill this thing right here we need to make sure she dies for real," Marcus said.

"And then what? We go back to Mexico for more hiding?" a high Inez asked, walking into the kitchen, catching the last bit of their conversation. "And I ain't pulling no kind of trigger."

Byron was behind her with a needle in his hand. He looked just as high as she did.

"Good, because your ass can't shoot no fucking way," Li'l Crook joked.

Inez stuck up the middle finger. "Damn, that's a

lot of drugs!" she said, when her eyes met the possessions on the table.

"And you ain't getting none! You stupid fiend!" Byron cackled.

"Marcus, that sure is a lot of drugs!" Inez said again, this time with even more awe.

"Yeah, I know. Y'all take this shit to the back. I don't want blood getting over it when I blow her fuckin' face off," Marcus said. He aimed the gun at her mouth and pulled it away slowly.

Li'l Crook, Cadillac, Byron, and Inez gathered the drugs and carried them to the back bedroom.

Kentia was left alone in the kitchen with Marcus. She quickly constructed an escape plan in seconds and proceeded to take immediate action.

She grabbed the glass jar of what looked like sugar, but was actually salt, and threw it in Marcus' face. He squealed like a girl. She ran out of the kitchen and then out of the front door.

The last thing she heard was Marcus calling for his backup and footsteps chasing behind her.

Linking Disaster

Theori drove to Jayshaun's house, her new home since her brush with death. When Jayshaun heard about what happened to Theori, he went up to the hospital and apologized for their roller coaster past. He offered her a stay in his place until she could find another place to stay. Theori, who always had love for Jayshaun throughout their ups and downs, was glad he made the turnaround. While she recovered in the hospital, Jayshaun and his boys removed her things from the old apartment.

Jayshaun never had the chance to seek revenge on Theori's attempted murderers because local Compton rumors had it that they hid out in Mexico, and there was no telling if they were coming back anytime soon. Crook was so slick and tricky that Jayshaun couldn't capture him. Crook knew Jayshaun was seeking to kill him and stayed off the Compton scene.

Recently, nights at the house were spent arguing on revenge. Theori wanted to handle it in court, and Jayshaun wanted to handle it on the streets.

"Jayshaun, don't worry about it. They got what's coming to them," Theori said.

Jayshaun argued, "Hell nah, man. It ain't coming fast enough. Just one round will do it. On Cedar Block Piru, they asses are mine when I see them!"

"Jayshaun," Theori replied, "boy, don't trip. I got my lawyer and police on top of it."

Jayshaun shook his head. "Theori, are you really depending on the fucking police to catch them? Woman, police drop homicide cases like they drop their drawers to shit! They just glad you're alive because that makes you one less statistic. You'd be lucky if the cops weren't involved in that shit! Damn, those fools are lucky I can't find them. It's a wrap once I find out they're back running in Compton."

Theori shook her head, hoping it wouldn't turn into one of those repeated nights, and made a turn onto Cedar. She pulled up in front of the house and thanked God she made it home safely. She got out of the car and approached the front door.

Jayshaun was there to open it for her. He gently pulled her in, stuck his head outside the door and looked around the perimeter. He came back inside, closing the door behind him.

Theori saw Murder and Romeo on the couch locking and loading guns. She turned around and looked at Jayshaun, who was holding a pistol of his own.

"What the hell is going on?" she asked fearfully.

"Relax, baby," Jayshaun answered. "We found out Crook's people are back from Mexico."

"Where are they? In Compton? Staying where?" Theori asked in a rush.

"Calm down, baby. My boy Sean said he saw that Mickey bitch stripping at Eye Candy this afternoon."

"So she went back to stripping?"

"Don't worry about that. I'm sending you to my cousin's house 'cuz shit is about to get real hot over here."

"Where does your cousin stay?" Theori asked.

"In Torrance," Jayshaun responded. "Don't trip. I'm gonna have Romeo take you there."

"Jayshaun, no! I can call my lawyer and the police. We'll have them get on their trail again!" Theori pleaded. "Don't do anything crazy, please!"

"Why you so in love with the police? Huh? Girl, this is Compton, not Beverly Hills. You got to do shit for yourself!" Jayshaun said.

Theori sucked her teeth. "As much as they lock young, Black men up in jail, I'm sure they'll be right on it," she said, adding sarcasm.

"Romeo, she's ready to go," Jayshaun said, looking Theori straight in the eye. "Go to the car."

"No," Theori replied firmly.

"I'm only asking you one more time. Don't let me have to pick you up and carry you out," Jayshaun said, just as firm.

Knowing he meant what he said and was determined to get his way regardless of what she wanted, Theori headed outside toward the car. Romeo followed her out.

They got in the car and headed west toward Torrance. Romeo was going down Alameda Street toward Rosecrans Avenue. He turned left and punched on the accelerator.

The need to drive fast was unknown, but Theori hoped he would slow down for the young lady running across Rosecrans. "ROMEO-STOP!" she hollered.

He screeched to a halt, and the girl was slightly hit by the bumper of the car. She fell to the ground, legs tired from running from Long Beach Boulevard to Santa Fe Avenue. Still, the pain of running two blocks for safety didn't stop her.

She got up and turned to see if the three men were still chasing after her. They were a block away.

Theori looked in their direction and immediately recognized what was going on. "Oh shit!" she whispered. She quickly got out of the car and grabbed the young girl.

"Get the fuck off me!" she screamed, trying to break free.

"Chill out! I'm tryin'a help! Get in the car!" Theori yelled.

She refused.

One of the men fired off a gun, and the bullet shattered the back window of the car, barely missing Romeo's head.

"Fuck that bitch, Theori, let's go!" Romeo said, ready to do seventy miles per hour to get away from the shooters.

The girl acted as if she recognized Theori and said, "Oh damn, you're Theori?"

Two more shots fired and echoed the streets of Compton. That sent the two women flying into the back seat, cutting up their arms from the shattered glass.

Romeo sped off, to escape losing another window, or losing a life.

"What's your name?" Theori asked as Romeo made a sharp right turn onto Willowbrook Avenue.

"Kentia."

"Kentia, excuse my language, but what the fuck are you doing running in the streets of Compton?"

Kentia began to cry and shuddered with fear. How in the world did she get herself into this much trouble? It was the stupid decisions she made, as always. "I was making a delivery to some asshole named Marcus. Then he told me I was in the middle of some deadly beef between my boss and Crook."

"Marcus and Crook?"

"You're Theori. They mentioned how they tried to kill you, but you lived," Kentia said like a tattletale.

"Yeah, they did try to kill me. Police are looking for them. Were three of the men named Li'l Crook, Byron, and Lac with him?"

"Yup, and some light-skinned mixed girl," Kentia said.

"Damn it!" Theori cursed. "Romeo, you gotta go back to the crib now!"

"No, I have to get to LA. Normandie and Thirty-seventh! I have to see my boss and tell him what happened," Kentia said.

"Honey, I'm trying to save your life. Look, I have to call the police," Theori said.

"I don't want no part in this! I need to get to my

side of town. I'm going to get kicked out of the house if I don't reach my boss! Me and my girl!"

"Well, at least let me get you to somewhere safe so you can get cleaned up. Our arms look like we're suicidal teens! I'll take you home, but not in this busted-back window ride, okay? Do you have anywhere else you can go, since your boss is throwing you out?" Theori asked.

"No," Kentia sobbed. A look of realization came over her face as she remembered what The Boss told her. She and Stephanie were both out of the house. She could explain the situation with Crook to her boss and hopefully he'd show some mercy, but would he believe her? He had to.

She snatched the cell phone out of Theori's hand and dialed up her boss's number. "Derek! It's Kentia. Where's The Boss?" she asked. She was put on hold. The next voice she heard was that of her boss. "Boss, I got into some trouble."

"What kind of trouble?"

"Your trouble. That Marcus guy works for some guy named Crook. You knew him back in the day. They said this was payback for you taking a loan and walking out on him! They were going to kill me! I didn't get the drugs either! They're still at their apartment."

"Shit!"

This was the first time Kentia heard concern and worry in his voice.

"I knew I shouldn't have done business in Compton after that last girl." He mumbled it so low, Kentia could barely hear him.

"Huh?" Kentia asked, not sure of what his exact words were.

"Damn it! You safe? You cool? Where are you?" The Boss asked. *I can't believe Crook was going to take out one of my workers in order to get to me*, he thought.

"Yes. I'm with a friend. Do I still get to keep my job, sir?" Kentia asked. She added, "Even though I was set up and was supposed to get killed?"

"I don't know. We just lost fifty thousand dollars worth of drugs. That means my girls gotta work triple time, prices gotta go up, and wages gotta go down . . . all to replace my missing money."

"Boss, it wasn't my fault!"

"We'll talk about it later. Right now you need to get your ass out of Compton and back on this side of town!"

"Boss I—"

Click. He had hung up on her.

Kentia already knew her ass and Stephanie's ass was out of the house. The Boss was cruel, and even her brush with death wouldn't ease the fact he had lost a lot of money fooling with her.

"Everything okay?" Theori saw tears stream from Kentia's eyes.

"Yeah, sure! I only lost my home, my money, my pride, and my dignity! And I was almost killed tonight! I'm just grand!" she wailed.

"Girl, I lost all that about a month ago, but I got it back. And I was dealing with the same exact people," Theori shared with her.

"How?" Kentia inquired.

"Long story, and I'm alive to tell you. I'm calling the police," Theori answered. She called the cops and told them the suspects were back in Compton and mentioned where to find them.

Romeo went back to the house. All three of them, shaken and stirred, went into the house immediately. Theori saw that Jayshaun and Murder were chilling on the couch, apparently waiting for the clock to strike twelve.

"What the hell is going on?" Jayshaun asked.

Theori and Kentia both informed Jayshaun and Murder of what had just happened in the last fifteen minutes.

While Theori made the appointed dinner for Kirrah, she told Kentia the inspiring story of what had happened to her in the past two years. When she was done, Kentia told her about her story. They compared stories and struggles and learned a great deal from the other. Both found a bond that they knew would keep them close.

The Turnaround

Simone looked on as Benny massaged Kirrah's shoulders, as he did before every Affected seminar she conducted. A look of peace was written all over her face.

"Feeling better?" he asked her.

"Yes," Kirrah replied. "Oh Lord, where is this girl Kentia? Do you think she'll do it?"

On the drama-filled night the previous week, Kirrah had met Kentia at Theori's house and sympathized with her. Kirrah felt strongly that she would be a marvelous addition to the Affected team and offered her a spot on the team. Kirrah wanted to use Kentia immediately and asked if she could speak at the next seminar at Santa Monica High. Kentia was skeptical about it and was still doubtful to the day of the seminar.

"Hopefully," Simone said.

"I'm scared she will change her mind. You know how unsure she was about it. Where's her brother, Corey? I want him to make sure she's going to speak." Kirrah ran rapidly behind the stage of Santa Monica High School looking for him.

Benny found Corey before she did and told him they wanted him to make sure Kentia was going to go through with her speech.

Corey agreed to comfort Kentia. He went to the left side of the stage and gave her a hug.

"Hey, brother! Ain't this food good? I haven't eaten like this in a long time!" she said.

"If you woulda been in Momma's crib instead of the whorehouse, you would've been eating food better than this!" Corey said.

Kentia made a sad face.

"I'm sorry, sister. But they want to know—"

"Who are *they*?" Kentia asked, cutting him off.

"Kirrah, Simone, and Benny want to know if you are ready."

"I'm a bit nervous," Kentia admitted. "But I'm still going to do it. I'm not going to let the team down."

Kirrah stood right behind them to catch the answer. "I just know you're going to do great! Don't be nervous! Trust me, they'll relate to you. I know this for a fact." Kirrah patted Kentia's back.

Kentia shook her head nervously and said, "I sure hope so. But I'll do my best and won't let you down." She looked around at Kirrah, Simone, Benny, and Corey.

The only person missing was Theori. She had to be in court for the trial of Marcus, Li'l Crook, Cadillac, Byron, and Inez for attempted murder and rape. It was a given that they were getting locked up for years to come.

In the next few days she would find out Crook was murdered in his club on the same night Jayshaun came in the house with a wide ear-to-ear smile on his face.

"Are you ready? Simone is about to call you out there, sweetie," Kirrah said, combing a piece of Kentia's hair behind her ears.

"Almost . . . no, I guess I am. I have no choice now, do I?"

"No, you don't." Kirrah laughed. "All right, let's go!"

"NO, WAIT!" called two recognizable voices.

Kentia ran to them and took them both in her arms. "Shanti! Stephanie! What are y'all doing here?"

"Girl, we saw the flyer on the counter and said, 'We want in on this too!' Are you about to speak?" Stephanie asked.

After Kentia and Stephanie were kicked out of The Boss' house, Shanti once again opened up her home to them. Kentia didn't want to live with Shanti at first, but Stephanie really needed a place to stay. Kentia did get over her pride and moved in with Shanti, along with Stephanie. Stephanie had a newfound joy in her and was also working toward getting her son back in her care.

"Oh, I'm so glad you came! You guys, this is my friend Kirrah. Kirrah, these are my best friends, Shanti and Stephanie," Kentia said excitedly, introducing the girls to each other.

They shook hands. Shanti said, "Okay, girl, we'll leave you alone. You better do your thing, girl, and represent! Make Mama proud!"

Shanti, Stephanie, and Corey left backstage and took their seats in the crowded auditorium.

At last, Simone introduced Kentia in a sweet and very flattering introduction.

Kentia made her way to the front of the stage. She gazed out at the faces of over a hundred girls. They were all beautiful, and their eyes told stories she could relate to, and some she could not.

She began confidently, "My name is Kentia Bradford. I'm from Los Angeles and I graduated from Crenshaw High. I'm twenty-two years old but I got one hell—I mean, heck of a story to tell. I had a love for luxury, the finer things in life. I loved cash more than I cherished my life, and it almost got me killed. You couldn't tell me nothing! Guys looked at me and said, 'I ain't sayin' she's a gold digger' . . . but I was."

About the Author

Erica Kimberly Barnes was born and raised in Los Angeles, California. She realized at a young age she wanted to be an author. At age fifteen, her family moved to Indiana to be closer to family. A year later, the family relocated to Virginia. Though the move from one side of the nation to the other was difficult to adjust to as a teenager, it only strengthened her love for writing.

During her senior year in high school, Erica wrote *I Ain't Sayin' She's A Gold Digger*. She was blessed with her first book deal with Qboro Books soon after.

After graduating from high school, Erica moved back to California. The Los Angeles native enjoys reading, hanging out with friends, and writing.

You can reach her at:
miss.ericak@hotmail.com

Immortal

BY ERICA BARNES

Chapter Six—Dior

She nervously looked at her cell phone, wondering why he had not called her back yet. As told to do, she called him at four, an hour after he got off work. He should have been home by now. After four missed calls and a voice mail, Dior's phone should've been ringing with Calvin's name and picture blinking on the screen. It was approaching the fifth hour and doubt seemed to take over.

Never getting over insecurity in her relationship, Dior let it get the better of her. Fears of Calvin cheating or even talking to another girl clouded her brain. She gently placed her cell phone on the desk of her dorm room.

Shay entered the dorm room they shared and saw the look of worry on her best friend's face. "What happened?" she asked, assuming the couple was going through the monthly turmoil.

"Nothing. He just hasn't called me yet. And it feels weird."

"You got an intuition or something?" Shay asked.

"I don't know. Can an intuition be wrong?"

"I would think so, but usually it's not," Shay answered. "You think Calvin is cheating on you? It may not be intuition. It's probably insecurity. You tend to do that often, Dior."

"Well, Calvin made me this way. I don't think he knows I know. But he has cheated on me before. How do I know he's not going to do it again?"

"You don't," Shay replied.

"So what am I supposed to do?"

Shay shrugged and got into her bed. "I'm taking a nap. Wake me up when it's time to eat."

Dior agreed to do so as she grabbed the dorm phone. She dialed the number to Calvin's house phone.

"Hello? Calvin?"

"No, Dior. It's Khalid," I said, in a groggy voice. I was 'sleep on the couch when I heard the phone ring. "You're looking for your man?"

"Yes, I am," she said forwardly.

I heard worry in her voice. From that, I knew she was coming out with a series of questions after I told her he wasn't at the house.

"He's not here yet," I answered, preparing myself for the 'reasonable-doubt' questions that were boarding her brain.

"Khalid, can I ask you a few questions?"

"Shoot," I allowed her. I pretended that this "questionnaire" was sudden, but I'd studied Dior and her position in the relationship, so her moves were predictable.

"Does Calvin have females calling the house?"

"No," I lied. "At least not when I pick up the

phone," when in actuality, three other females called for Calvin, but they were friends. I knew that for sure.

"Hmmm," Dior moaned. "I find that hard to believe. Has he told you about any experiences with other women?"

C'mon Dior, if it was him asking the questions I wouldn't rat you out, I thought. I fibbed, "No, he didn't, Dior."

She sucked her teeth. "Well, do you think Calvin is cheating?"

Not anymore, I wanted to say. But I couldn't! If Dior found out Calvin used to cheat, not that her common sense hadn't already told her, it wasn't going to be from my mouth. "Nah, I think he's crazy about you. If he ain't at work or with you, then he's at Evan's house. What could he and Evan possibly do? All they do is smoke and play video games," I stated what I knew . . . or at least what I hoped was true.

"You can't be too sure."

"Obviously, neither can you."

Dior, if I'm not mistaken, sobbed and blew her nose.

"What's that supposed to mean?"

"Why are you so insecure?" I asked.

"How many times have I heard that before?" she asked herself out loud.

"And how many times have you been honest?" I decided to throw in for more realization.

She answered, "I don't mean to be insecure. I really don't mean to be insecure. I really don't! But I can't afford to have him cheat on me again."

"Again?"

"Yes, again. I know he's cheated on me before."

"How did you find out?"

"It was when I was doing my senior year in Texas. High school years," Dior responded. "I don't want to go through that again. I really don't want to."

I felt sorry for her. I knew this was why she allowed herself to become Calvin's every necessity. By stepping down from her given authority, she hoped to keep Calvin from running around. Many guys would love to have a young woman like Dior who abided by their rules. But at what cost? And why must the woman pay?

"Khalid? You there?"

I had spaced out for about a couple of seconds. She had gotten lonely. "Yes, I am. Look, Dior, I know for a fact Calvin loves you. He ain't cheating. Is he showing any signs?"

"None that is for certain. It's little stuff, like not calling me back when he says or when he's supposed to," Dior answered.

"Okay, well, people get sidetracked. You know that. Use common sense over insecurity. It's bad if people notice it from the outside."

"All right."

"And another thing, don't let Calvin talk to you like you're a little kid. It's not cool the way he comes at you," I said. I felt it necessary to inform her about it. It bothered me to see another young man, especially my friend, talk down to their woman.

"I don't think he means to talk to me like that. He just gets angry, you know?"

"No, I don't know because I don't talk to a

woman like that no matter how mad I am. And don't tell me what you think. You're blind to it because you're in love with Calvin. You're so in love that you'd do anything for him," I said.

She snickered. "Well, excuse me. Somebody should receive the 'Tupac of the Year' award!"

"I can't help the fact that I respect all females, no matter where they come from or where they're going. And some of them don't deserve to be respected at all, now do they? I replied. "Now promise me that you will stand up for yourself and grow some heart!"

Dior laughed, and it warmed me to know I made her smile at a time it was needed.

"You got my word!" she said.

Timing is everything. Right when I was going to end the conversation, Calvin walked in the door. "What a coincidence! Here's Calvin." I tossed him the phone.

He caught it and put it to his cheek. "Hello?"

"Hey, boo!" Dior chimed. "Where ya been?"

"Evan's," Calvin answered.

"Shoulda known. You didn't pick up your cell when I called. Why?" Dior asked.

"I was playing *Madden*," Calvin said.

"Why didn't you call after you lost?" she asked, trying to add humor to the situation only she felt serious.

"We went to smoke. What were you and Khalid talking about?" Calvin asked, changing the subject. He trailed into the room.

"Nothing. I just called," Dior lied.

"You sure?"

"Um . . . yeah."

"Why does the phone indicate that ya'll been talking for seven minutes?"

"Calvin?"

"What were y'all talking about?"

"Nothing really. Just college."

"College? For Khalid?"

"No, he was asking me how things were going at San Bernadino."

Calvin was skeptical, but didn't let it faze him. "Right, Dior. If I'm not here when you call, just hang up. You understand me?"